At three forty-five p.m., the ER secretary
heard the first call on
the ambulance radio. An explosion in the filled
auditorium of Sinclair College,
practically adjacent to All Saints,
had knocked out a wall. When it happened,
the secretary and others in the nurses' station
felt the percussion and heard the blast.
There could be dozens of casualties.
Sirens whined and a cloud of gray smoke
drifted skyward...

T. B. KERR

ART & ARTifact

ART & ARTIFACT

See the author's website at http://xraystories.blogspot.com
Available through online retailers.
Published by the author.

ACKNOWLEDGEMENTS

Thank you,

Carolyn, my wife, for her great suggestions, stenography
and tolerance.
Mary, my sister, for her help.
And a special thanks to Yonathan, my good friend for trusting
me enough to give me the insights for the creation of
Tesfaye Ababa.

Dedicated to my Radiography colleagues.

Prologue

Tesfaye Ababa had a panicky feeling that intensified with each passing day. The escalating battle that raged in the nearby mountains affected everyone's lives including his. Any day now, twelve-year-old Tesfaye would have to leave his aunt's home to make the dangerous journey back to his mother's town. Summer break was almost over. And as much as he was anxious about the trip itself, he was afraid the school year would start without him.

Tesfaye sat at the wooden kitchen table in his aunt's house drawing a map by the light of a kerosene lantern. But the map wasn't of a real place. It didn't represent the geography of the mountainous farm region that surrounded him. And it didn't include the Blue Nile or Great Rift Valley that Ethiopia was

1

famous for. It was the pretend kind of map that kids make, with islands and jungles, pyramids and castles.

As he outlined the curving rivers of his make-believe map, Tesfaye's thoughts flowed away from the imminent trip he would soon have to make. With zigzag marks, he sketched a burning volcano at the top of the drawing, its lava flowing into the sea. His pencil described each shoreline with light strokes at first and then traced over heavier with a stronger commitment. Tesfaye's concentration ended with a thundering series of booms that seemed closer to the house than ever before.

Now gunfire and bomb blasts echoed across the rugged valley more frequently. Tesfaye heard his aunt call for his cousins to come inside. The lights didn't come on that afternoon at five o'clock as they usually did; the electricity had been cut. For a twelve-year-old, that meant no TV that night at the village center. For Tesfaye's aunt with a houseful of family, it meant hardship and danger. An Army ambulance blared its two-toned siren. Through the window, Tesfaye saw a neighbor pulling a stubborn donkey away from the road. Communist government troops barrelled past the house in brown trucks and tanks. The rebels advanced, coming down from the mountains. Dusk fell quickly into absolute darkness.

"*Tolo bel, Tesfaye. Tolo bel!*" His aunt yelled urgently in Amharic for Tesfaye to hurry. The time had come. He gathered his things immediately. A minibus about to arrive would take him and two cousins toward the town of Kombolcha where his mother lived. With a hasty good-bye for his family and payment made to the driver, they boarded the minibus.

Rocket and mortar fire shot across the night sky. Rebel forces pounded government troops into retreat. The battle lines and the bloodshed drew closer. Explosions rocked the hillsides and trees burned like torches. The minibus steered away and extinguished its lights for safety. Any lighted vehicle was a target. Slowly the minibus bounced down the sloped unpaved road, dodging villagers who walked in darkness. Having a flashlight or a lantern was just too risky. Out of a dirty window, all Tesfaye could make out was the silhouette of black peaks and occasional flashes of orange light. He knew people were dying. He remembered how his cousin was killed in a fuel tank explosion. Tesfaye thought maybe they should have stayed longer with his aunt. At least he was on his way, away from the fighting. He would see his mother again soon; he could only wish.

Abruptly at a crossroad by the base of a steep hill, the minibus was halted. Two soldiers approached the vehicle warily, gripping their Kalashnikov rifles. They could drive no farther. A dozen passengers, including Tesfaye and his older cousins, climbed out with their belongings in plastic bags and began to walk. Ahead of them lay a long dirt road visible only for several meters. The troops offered no resistance as the group, mainly children and women, passed on foot without speaking.

Tesfaye wasn't sure how long it would take to complete the nighttime passage. He knew it would be several kilometers. They walked far ahead of advancing rebel forces going in the same direction. The warm night air smelled of smoke. Now and then an ambulance or tank raced by. But they couldn't walk on the road's shoulder. That would risk being blown to bits by disturbing a land mine. Large craters fringed with rocks and debris proved that.

Despite repeated warnings from his cousins, Tesfaye and another boy raced downhill ahead of the others. With a burst of speed, Tesfaye tried to overcome his friend and then stumbled forward, hands flung out to break the fall. He heard his arm crack as he struck the dirt. Searing pain emanated from his wrist. In a matter of seconds, his excited anticipation of completing the trek had vanished. Panic and self-doubt overwhelmed him now. Fatigue eventually replaced intense pain. He felt so tired that he worried he would have to stop walking, left behind in the dark, war-torn countryside.

Tesfaye slowly tested his wrist. He could move it, but not without pain. He tried to contain his tears as his cousins helped

3

him get started again. Believing that some horrible fate would become of him should he fall behind, Tesfaye stoically trudged on. He mechanically placed one foot in front of the other.

-o-

In the early morning hours, Tesfaye stood in his mother's home again, in his mother's arms again.

"Egzyabehare yemasegen! Egzyabehare yemasegen baselam Darasek," his mother thanked God for his safe arrival. *"Dahena nehe?"* She asked if he was okay as she hugged him.

"Dahena nege tineshe dakemonial," Tesfaye answered that he was just a little tired. But in truth, his wrist ached. His mother knew he was actually exhausted. She got a piece of cardboard and an old cloth and wrapped his arm so that his wrist couldn't bend. Tesfaye told the story of his journey and relayed the details of his injurious fall as his mother sat on the edge of his bed. She reassured him that a doctor would check his wrist in the morning.

The sun was well above the plateau's horizon when Tesfaye awoke the next day. Breakfast included *kita*, a bread, which he dipped in oil and salt. While he ate, he gazed out the window and wondered what his friends were doing now.

Later, on the walk to a hospital clinic with his mother, Tesfaye ran into two friends he hadn't seen since last spring. They teased him about the makeshift splint his mother had put on the night before and talked about the pending start of middle school.

Continuing on their way, Tesfaye asked his mother one question after another about what the doctor at the clinic would do to his injured arm. In spite of being tired from the long trip the night before, he enjoyed walking down the roads with his mom. But he wasn't thrilled about their destination. In fact, he was frightened that he would see people who had been blown up or otherwise mutilated by the war.

When they came around the street corner and entered the low-rise cement block structure, Tesfaye inadvertently held his breath from the tension. His wrist pain worsened markedly as they went up to the reception desk. It felt like a nail was driven into it. He stood at the desk mystified when he heard the Russian triage nurse there speaking in Amharic, the official Ethiopian language. The Soviets supported the socialist government, pouring millions of dollars into it. The United States was giving support to the rebels for what amounted to a proxy war against the Soviet Union.

In the waiting room, patients including a crying two-year old, an emaciated old woman with a white headscarf and a one legged man distracted Tesfaye from his own discomfort.

After a while, the Russian nurse directed them to an exam room. The smell of alcohol in the sterile white room unnerved Tesfaye. It reminded him of malaria shots he had years before.

After another long wait, his wrist was x-rayed by a talkative technologist also speaking in Amharic with a Russian accent. A kind young doctor in a lab coat came in afterwards and showed Tesfaye his wrist on the films. Fortunately, he only had a minor fracture of his radius, but Tesfaye still needed a cast on his wrist. Holding his x-ray up to the light, Tesfaye was mesmerized. *So this is what my bones look like inside,* he thought. He studied the shapes and wondered how x-rays were made.

After the nurse put the cast on, they left for home with Tesfaye carrying his films and complaining the whole way about the itchiness across his left wrist. Still, he enjoyed every minute of his mother's attention as well as that of the Russian healthcare workers.

Addis Ababa, Ethiopia

"*Quaswan mita, mita,*" the teenage boys called out to pass the soccer ball. Tesfaye, now in high school, for the first time had a ball that actually bounced. Previous balls were handmade assemblages of rags, paper, and even mud. When he was younger, Tesfaye would make a ball filled with mud and rock to be used as a practical joke on unsuspecting kickers. Now that he had a good ball, it was ironic that he had little time to use it.

5

The countdown had begun. His father had made all the arrangements. In a matter of weeks they would leave Ethiopia with his stepmother to live in America. America the glamorous, he thought, the home of Hollywood, the place where the future is now, where everyone gets rich. They had won the chance to emigrate to the U. S. in a lottery. Instead of being refugees of war or famine, Tesfaye's family would be coming over simply as immigrants seeking better economic opportunity. After the fall of Ethiopia's communist dictatorship, the dream of coming to America had become real again. The downside for Tesfaye would be years spent away from his mother, grandmother, a brother and so many other relatives.

Though high school in Addis Ababa went well, he hoped that education in America would offer him more, more chances to improve his English and to attend college as his parents had. He focused on his studies in these last weeks to distract himself from the uncertainty that lie ahead.

It was a calm gathering of extended family that came to the airport that day in Addis Ababa. They were there to bid farewell to Tesfaye, his father and stepmother. A sweet, sad, but exciting day, Tesfaye for the first time viewed his life as a continuing journey, a one way trip through time with painful goodbyes along with promises of better things to come.

Far Rockaway, Queens, New York

What Tesfaye saw first in America perplexed him. Blocks and blocks of shabby houses went as far as the eye could see. Bridge posts rusted and poor looking people sat out on stoops in front of old apartment buildings. He felt quiet discouragement. This wasn't what he hoped to see in the famous city of New York. An aunt they were staying with told Tesfaye to be patient.

"Tesfaye, just wait, wait until tomorrow. Tomorrow, we'll go into Manhattan and you'll see the real New York. You know, like the World Trade Center, and all those great buildings. And then we'll drive up to Central Park," she said encouragingly.

Relieved by what he did see the following day, Tesfaye though couldn't help but wonder which end of the city he would end up at, the top, or the bottom.

With one year of high school remaining, Tesfaye gradually grew more acclimated to this new culture. It took a while to get used to the longer school days than he had in Addis Ababa. Tesfaye also had to use English in all his classes – not just in English class. One thing he had going for him was that his father had been an English grammar teacher back home, and this helped immensely. However, halfway through the school year his father decided to move to Rochester with his wife. Tesfaye's father had other relatives there, and on a visit, realized he wanted to get out of the city. Finding a factory job in Rochester made the decision to move easier. Plans were made for Tesfaye to continue living with his aunt and uncle until he joined his dad in the summer.

Tesfaye got a job at a little Italian market on the upper east side of Manhattan working weekends. During the long subway rides to work from Queens, Tesfaye would study as much as he could. Scanning the variety of peoples on the train, he began to think that all America was so diverse. In the little spare time he had, he would walk the beach near his uncle's apartment and squint out to at the blurred line where the ocean meets the sky. He wondered how long it would take a ship to make it to Africa from there.

One day after class in the high school cafeteria, Tesfaye continued painting the thick-lined African style mural he had been working on for months. Drawing had always been a hobby of his; the quiet, contemplative nature of artwork suited his personality well. So when the school sought volunteers for the large project, he took on the challenge. As Tesfaye worked, white and Latino students passed by without stopping. They offered loud compliments. A group of mostly black basketball players also yelled encouraging remarks. Tesfaye considered himself, as an Ethiopian, one of a distinct and blended people, referred to as *Habish*, meaning mixed. Without being aware of it, Tesfaye had found through his artwork, his own way to adjust and fit in to this sometimes-puzzling new world. He poured some black paint with white paint into a pail to create a mid-range tone that he would use for a final but essential portion of the design.

Later on, Tesfaye cleaned the gray paint off his long-handled brush and wrapped it in a rag. He went through his mental list of things he still had to do before moving to Rochester to attend college. Tesfaye felt satisfaction that he was putting the finishing touches on both the mural and the school year. And although in many ways over the past year Tesfaye had to constantly adapt, these were just the first steps in his search for an identity in America.

Chapter 1

August 24th All Saints Hospital, Seven Years Later

While gently lifting the patient's unaffected leg onto a stepstool, Tesfaye Ababa attempted to explain to the patient exactly what he was doing.

"You see, Mrs. Sheehan, I must move your 'good' leg out of the way to x-ray the hip that hurts you." Tesfaye's struggles with English worked its way into every aspect of his life, not the least of which was his exchanges with patients.

"Whatever you say, but please, please tell me this is the last one," said the sixty-five year old patient as she firmly gripped the edges of the x-ray table. Ironically, she had fallen in a hospital elevator while visiting her sick husband and now found herself in the emergency department. In the few minutes Tesfaye had spent with her, he realized that this woman was not only in a great deal of pain but also on the verge of an emotional breakdown.

"After I shoot this x-ray, I'll know if it's the last one," answered Tesfaye.

"So then you'll tell me if it's broken?"

"No, I'm sorry. The doctor will talk to you after he looks at the x-rays."

Tesfaye aligned the x-ray tube to shoot horizontally toward the woman's opposite groin. He told the patient to hold still then walked behind the leaded glass window to press the exposure button.

Now sporting a thin goatee, wearing green scrubs and filled out to a grown man's proportions, Tesfaye continued to improve the skills that took him three years of college to obtain. Being a necessary part of a medical team gave him real satisfaction. He appreciated that his knowledge of body structures could be applied in a meaningful way. This was his first "real job" in America and Tesfaye, for the most part, enjoyed the interactions with colleagues at All Saints Hospital.

Tesfaye returned the patient's leg to a more comfortable position and then checked the hip x-ray on the workstation monitor. A sub-capital fracture, he thought as he heard Ron Koharski, his brawny coworker for the evening shift, enter the room.

"Come on, Ababa. Aren't you done yet? I just shot four portable chests while you dilly-dally with this one hip," complained Koharski, adjusting his ID badge on his black scrub top.

"I'm finished with her. Can you help me to move her back to her cart?"

"Yeah, after I throw these cassettes on the digitizer, buddy," replied Koharski, now standing over Tesfaye's shoulder, peering down at the image monitor. "Nice little hip fracture there. Probably gonna need a total hip replacement with all that arthritis," remarked Koharski loudly. Tesfaye cringed; he thought there was a good chance his patient heard Koharski's comment.

Tesfaye prepared the woman for the return back to her ER room. As he aligned the cart with the x-ray table, Koharski came up to assist with the transfer.

"So, did I break my leg or not? Because it sure feels terrible."

"Ah, don't worry, the surgeons fix these all the time," replied Koharski as the two techs slid her onto the cart.

"Surgery! You mean I need surgery? I can't! My husband — who will take care of my husband — he's got cancer. No! I can't believe this is happening!" She covered her eyes with her hand as she sobbed heavily. Koharski walked away shaking his head as Tesfaye pushed the cart through the doorway. Tesfaye consoled her as best he could. He wished Koharski had kept his big mouth shut but it was too late now.

When Tesfaye finished x-ray school in Rochester where he lived with his father, he sought and found a job in Buffalo, about seventy miles away. Moving to Buffalo enabled him to further his education at the University at Buffalo, where a degree in Geography was offered.

The Buffalo area looked different than Rochester to him, older, more urban but with some great architecture. In contrast, Rochester seemed more park-like, greener and more open. Within Buffalo, Tesfaye soon realized that South Buffalo was a unique entity of its own kind. It was the last large section of the city that was predominately white and populated by the grown children of steelworkers and factory workers, fireman and policeman, bar owners and patrons. The railroads and highways apparently separated South Buffalo from the rest of the city in more than a physical sense.

All Saints Hospital stood above its surrounding South Buffalo homes, taverns and delicatessens for over one hundred years. Tesfaye sensed the history each time he walked through the refurbished lobby with its expansive blue, green and gold stained-glass design of Jesus the shepherd surrounded by his flock. The deep crimson walls were covered with large portraits of several Catholic saints and apostles as well as local priests and nuns who had dedicated themselves to the care of the sick, elderly and orphaned. Studying the varnished portrait of St. Lawrence one day, Tesfaye then read the accompanying panel. He grimaced when he came to the part that said: *"…upon the orders of Emperor Valerian, Lawrence was executed by means of burning on a red-hot gridiron."*

Many of the women and men at All Saints Hospital not only worked there, but were also born there. And some would take their last breaths in its wings. Tesfaye needed only a few weeks of work to see All Saints as a small village within a town within a still larger city.

When Tesfaye came back to the ER x-ray room after returning the woman with the hip fracture, he sat at the computer to complete documentation of the procedure. Meanwhile, Koharski began a lumbar spine series on a woman who had fallen down her basement stairs.

Kevin Collins, an older coworker with thinning hair, stopped by to see where his next patient was.

"Hey, Tesfaye, how's the night going down here in the pit?"

"Not too bad, man. Are you guys busy in CAT Scan?"

"You know, it's always busy in CT. And when it's not, it's only because we're waiting for the transporters to bring us the next one," said Kevin, removing his glasses to rub his eyes. Kevin Collins and most other radiologic technologists at All Saints were cross-trained in Computed Tomography. Tesfaye had worked many shifts in the ER with Kevin and they had a good rapport.

"Can you do me a favor?" Kevin asked. "When Ron is done with that patient, call me in CT, so that I can scan her."

"No problemo, amigo." In addition to Geography classes, Tesfaye also had taken some Spanish. Before Kevin left, he invited Tesfaye over to his house for a cookout that weekend. Tesfaye said to "count him in" and returned to the computer.

12

Koharski called over to Tesfaye, "Hey, what did your girlfriend Collins want?"

"Oh, he wants that patient when you're done."

"Okay. He can have her. She's a frequent flyer. You know, one of our regular scum—I mean—clients. I probably have x-rayed her a hundred fifty times."

Chapter 2

In the breakroom of the hospital radiology department, the personnel changed from second to third shift. Iptesaam Abdullah, a mother of five, greeted the second shifters as she put her lunch in the fridge. Iptesaam, called Saam, had married at age fifteen. The traditional black headscarf she wore contrasted her casual green scrubs. Saam enjoyed working with Tesfaye. She thought he had a better understanding of Muslims than the others since Tesfaye had grown up in Africa.

Around the circular table strewn with magazines sat three second shift techs with their purses ready to clock out. Stephanie and Jane toyed with their cell phones while Megan bit her nails. Off to one side stood Willie Stiles, a radiology transporter and new father at the age of sixty. When Tesfaye came into the room the young women glanced up.

"Yo Tesfaye, when you coming out with us?" asked Stephanie. Tesfaye smiled, saying hello.

"What's the matter? Afraid of us girls?"

"Hey, Tes, I know somebody that might like you."

"Yeah, sounds good but I got to work tonight, maybe another time," answered Tesfaye diplomatically.

Tesfaye and Saam headed into the entrance lobby on the way to the ER x-ray room in the hospital's newest wing. With the gift shop, coffee cart and information desk closed for the night, there were only a few people left in the lobby, probably waiting for rides home. Stopping in the comfortable and warmly lit space for a moment, Tesfaye motioned for Saam to come closer to one of the saint portraits.

"Did you ever read this? It's really a sad story. Actually, it's pretty horrible. Go ahead and read it."

Saam read aloud from the placard next to the portrait of Saint Dymphna: *"Saint Dymphna, born in Ireland is a patron saint of the mentally ill. Her father fell madly in love with her, claiming he was overwhelmed by the resemblance that Dymphna bore to her deceased mother. He insisted they marry after her mother died. Dymphna refused and fled to the continent, devoting her life to Jesus. She became a martyr for Christ when her father found her in Belgium and beheaded her...* Wow, that's pretty bizarre."

"Yeah, for sure," replied Tesfaye.

They left the front lobby and, lightening the mood, Saam teased Tesfaye about eating ham on a previous night. Like the Muslims, Tesfaye's religion – Ethiopian Orthodox Christian — discouraged eating pork. They entered the emergency department in good spirits to begin the night shift.

"And every time I touch you, you just tremble inside..." Down in the ER x-ray room, Sean Muldoon sang along with Van Morrison's "Moondance" coming from the radio. He had a rich melodic voice. A few years ago he was the lead singer for a band.

It didn't last long though. After a night of flirting with a girl between sets, he got into a barfight and threw the girl's boyfriend through the huge front window. Muldoon ran out before the cops came. The big, curly red haired x-ray technologist munched on pretzel rods and clicked the computer mouse several times, thereby tracking his last x-ray case. He picked up the phone and dialed.

"*Melissa, it's Sean. I'm leaving here in five minutes; I'll be right over to pick you up…*" He took another pretzel rod and held it between his finger and thumb like a cigar, waiting for his turn to speak.

"*So what if it's late? You can sleep in tomorrow…*" Before taking a bite, Muldoon sucked the salt off it. Quickly, the pretzel disappeared into his chomping jaws.

"*What do my kids have anything to do with this?!…*He listened for a while and then took a swig of water from a styrofoam cup. Feeling his irritation grow, he interrupted Melissa.

"*You got to be kidding me! You're dumping me? Your old boyfriend is white trash! Melissa, he had his license revoked…*The cup was empty and he crushed it on the countertop under the phone.

"*I have my sources. Anyway, we'll work this out, you'll see. I'm coming right over!*" Exasperated, Muldoon swore as he slammed down the phone. At first he didn't seem to notice or care that Tesfaye and Saam had walked in as his relief.

"Look, the Third World's here!" barked Muldoon as he headed out the door. Then he poked his head back in.

"I see you left your camels and spears out in the hall."

"*Dahena edar*, Sean Muldoon. That means good night," said Tesfaye, playing along with Muldoon's foolishness.

"Good night, smart ass!" said Saam.

When Muldoon was gone, Tesfaye turned to Saam. "You know, they never let you forget, do they?"

"What do mean?" asked Saam.

"I mean these people; they never let you forget that you're from somewhere else. That they think you're different. I mean,

I've been in this country almost nine years and almost every day somebody says something to me about elephants or AIDS or starvation."

"Well, you know what, Tes? I was born here and I still have to hear it. But it doesn't bother me anymore. After a while, you'll get used to it too," claimed Saam as she adjusted her headscarf.

Tesfaye never really experienced being a victim of overt racism in America. For that, he felt in a strange way lucky.

"Maybe you're right about getting used to it. But you know what the funny thing is? The longer I'm in this country the more 'African' I feel. Like my roots just keep getting stronger."

Chapter 3

The next day in her parents' suburban home Melissa Adams, a petite hospital clerk, prepared a spartan lunch of tuna, lettuce and flavored water. Melissa never really had a great appetite, and a poor night's sleep only made it worse. She cut her sandwich into diagonal halves and sat at the butcher-block kitchen table with the Sunday comics. Her cell phone vibrated on her hip. Melissa prayed it wasn't Sean Muldoon.

She met Sean in the cafeteria at All Saints when her friend Megan, an x-ray tech, introduced them. It was an introduction both young women now regretted. Melissa checked the caller ID. Of course, she thought, it's him again. As she answered the call, she promised herself it would be the last time she ever spoke to him.

"...Sean, I told you. It's over...No!...I don't want to see you anymore!" she exclaimed, then disconnected him.

Their dating had lasted only a few awful weeks. At a Fantasy Football party at his friend's house, he drank too much. At a "gentleman's club" that he took her to, Sean obviously knew the dancers well, and he drank too much there also. And finally, at a hunting club party in the woods with his dad, Sean ignored his young daughters and drank even more. Melissa couldn't take it any longer. Especially disturbing to her was that he left his little daughters without supervision at that outdoor party. Now that Melissa had cut him loose, she kept getting phone messages from him that had taken a turn from nasty to threatening. Then a familiar pain radiated again from her abdomen. She shoved the plate of food aside. Repeated visits to her doctor yielded no diagnosis. She doubled over in the chair and then melted to the floor with knees drawn to her chest. Her mother ran into the kitchen, saw Melissa there, turned her face-up and prepared to take her to the ER at All Saints Hospital.

12:45 p.m.

In the afternoon, Tesfaye arrived at Kevin's house. A row of blue Rose of Sharon lined the driveway in a late summer show. It was extremely hot and muggy, even for the African-born Tesfaye.

"I hope you brought your trunks," Kevin said, coming out from the yard.

"Trunks? What are trunks?"

"Your swim trunks, you know, a bathing suit."

"No, no, I didn't. You know, I don't even own any."

"Well, never mind. Come on back." Kevin urged.

Kevin's wife greeted Tesfaye. Kevin's kids, two boys, ran through the yard.

"Kev, you got a big yard. You know what you should do? You should plant some fruit trees or something."

"Fruit trees? I have enough trouble growing grass with all these weeds."

The boys jumped off the high wooden deck into the large round swimming pool. Tesfaye's eyes rested for a moment on clusters of black-eyed Susans and purple coneflowers by the patio.

"You can swim in your shorts if you want," said Kevin as he climbed the pool ladder. "Come on, I promise you'll enjoy it."

"Well…all right man. I'll give it a try," replied Tesfaye uncomfortably.

With more than a little trepidation, Tesfaye climbed the ladder to the top and peered down at what seemed like a bottomless blue circle of water. Ordinarily, he wouldn't have ventured even this far. But, because it was so hot and Kevin was a friend, he thought he should at least attempt it. At first, the water felt cool and refreshing. But Tesfaye lost his footing near the bottom of the ladder and went head first into the water. The boys laughed until they realized that Tesfaye struggled to get himself upright. Grabbing onto the siderail, he pulled himself up and started coughing. Tesfaye felt shaken, unnerved by his plunge and swallowing water. *If they only knew what this was like for me,* he thought.

After he recovered, Tesfaye laughed at himself. Kevin handed Tesfaye a bright green float.

"Try just floating first, and then maybe kicking."

"I don't know. I never learned to swim," admitted Tesfaye.

Just take it easy, Tesfaye told himself. He held his breath and swallowed his pride, but try as he may, Tesfaye couldn't relax in the water. It was a foreign environment to him, almost like an astronaut's first experience with weightlessness. Years ago, he came close to drowning when he fell into a water and debris-filled pit behind a hospital in Ethiopia. Dug deep and long for the burial of garbage, the pit contained paper and other treasures to a young boy. But the floating papers, cardboard and boxes disguised a filthy and dangerous broth produced by the rainy season and raw sewage. If it hadn't been for a woman collecting cactus nearby, the young Tesfaye may have not survived. She screamed and people from the hospital rescued him. After the filth was cleaned off and a doctor checked out Tesfaye, he was sent home, shaken but otherwise okay.

Tesfaye laid his chest now across the float but he couldn't balance himself. Each time it tipped he felt a strange sense of vertigo; not knowing which way was up. It seemed just plain unnatural to him to simply lift both his feet off the bottom. After repeated attempts, Tesfaye gave up.

Later, they enjoyed hamburgers and drinks on a small patio behind the house. Tesfaye studied the bees circling harmlessly around the pink flowers of the spireas. He watched as the boys came down the pool ladder. Then Tesfaye recalled how surprised he was when he saw dozens of backyard pools while landing at the Buffalo Niagara airport after a trip to Washington. He never would have guessed it by Buffalo's reputation as a blizzard factory.

"So, how was work last night?" Kevin asked.

"Okay, you know, same old stuff. A few MVAs, Muldoon yelling at his girlfriend on the phone, STAT portables and lots of abdomen x-rays."

"That sounds about right," remarked Kevin, reaching for a water bottle. "You probably won't be able to work those double shifts so much now that's school's starting. I don't know how you did so many this summer."

"One word. Stamina!" laughed Tesfaye. "Remember, my people are great marathon runners. You ever hear of Haile Gebrselassie?"

"Umm, no, not really."

"He was a famous Olympic runner, a record breaker. You know, there's a story about him. I think it was that he ran with a crooked arm because, for so many years, he ran to school with books under that arm," explained Tesfaye.

"And you have some of the same stamina?"

"Well, maybe for me it's my Ethiopian coffee."

"Right. That's more like it. Hey, what are you takin' this semester, anyway?" inquired Kevin.

21

"Let's see. I've got a cartography class, a Spanish class, one in Environmental Science and another in soil,"

"Soil?"

"Yeah, you know, earth. We test soil for its components and properties and then put the results on charts and stuff."

"Okay, I get it, the anatomy and physiology of dirt," joked Kevin.

"You could say that, I guess," said Tesfaye.

Tesfaye reminded Kevin of their weak attempts on a previous night to speak Spanish to a patient. Instead of asking the woman when *(cuando)* her last menstrual period was, Kevin asked where *(donde')* her last menstrual period was. The patient and the two techs had a good laugh over the simple but important error. When it was time to go, Tesfaye thanked Kevin and his wife, explaining that he had to work that night. He found solace in knowing that he had a friend in Buffalo who would open his home to him.

Chapter 4

Emergency Department Radiology Room

That night was more like a nightmare for Tesfaye. Muldoon pushed, yanked and manhandled patients all night long. Fuming over his breakup with his girlfriend Melissa, he carried on with vulgarities about what a lowlife he thought she was. Just two weeks ago, he proudly showed revealing cell phone photos to anyone who wanted a peek. Now that she had dumped him and returned to her old boyfriend, he was livid, and taking it out on any patient he could.

"What do you mean you don't know how you got wet?" Muldoon asked an incontinent old man. "I'll tell you how. You peed all over yourself," uttered Muldoon as he yanked the man off the x-ray table without waiting for Tesfaye's help.

"Man, you say some weird things to patients," said Tesfaye calmly. "You got to take it easy on these old people."

Muldoon barely acknowledged Tesfaye's remarks saying only, "We're too busy to be changing diapers here."

Then Sean Muldoon tucked the tormented man's blanket under his neck and with a saccharin-sweet voice said, "How's that George? Are you warm enough?"

A few minutes later Tesfaye began a shoulder x-ray series on a slim teenage football player. The kid got hurt in a practice game earlier that night, went home and was suffering ever since. Noting that the boy seemed a little unsteady, Tesfaye sat him on a stool at the x-ray board instead of having him stand.

"Okay. Now, I want you to turn your arm outward. Just move a little to your right. Good. Hold still," said Tesfaye and then went and pressed the exposure button. The boy put his head down before Tesfaye could position him for the next image. Sensing the kid may be about to pass out, Tesfaye quickly asked if he was all right and immediately got him a cool washcloth. Muldoon had returned to the room and came up alongside Tesfaye. Muldoon saw the boy and began to lecture the kid.

Muldoon bellowed, "Buddy, you gotta toughen up if you're gonna play football." Tesfaye and the teenager stared at Muldoon in disbelief. "What position do you play anyway?" Muldoon asked. Weakly, the kid told him "quarterback."

"You're looking at the starting quarterback of St. James the Great, four years straight and four championships," boasted Muldoon. The boy said nothing. Tesfaye moved in to complete the shoulder series.

"Now, if you're able, I'll turn your arm inwards as far as it will go," said Tesfaye. Seeing that the kid had no difficulty with the request, Tesfaye guessed it could be a clavicle fracture.

Muldoon bragged on and on about his football prowess in high school. In a way, Tesfaye pitied him. Muldoon finished high school thirteen years ago, Tesfaye estimated, and still talked about it as if it were last week. Tesfaye clicked on the mouse at the workstation and brought up the boy's first x-ray. An obvious mid-shaft clavicle fracture, thought Tesfaye. Muldoon disappeared from the room after mumbling something about the kid being a wuss. Tesfaye smiled to the kid, helped him stand, and walked him back to his bed in the next room.

Tesfaye didn't know where Muldoon went, and although that meant doing the work alone, he really didn't care. Luckily, Tesfaye thought, Muldoon hadn't seen his ex-girlfriend Melissa leaving the ER with her mother as he had. That could have been really ugly, he guessed. But then again, Muldoon could have just turned on the charm as he did at the most unexpected times.

Tesfaye hadn't seen Muldoon for at least forty minutes and figured the night would end like every night does, doing what he can and clocking out when his shift was done. Generally, Tesfaye was not one to check schedules to see whom he'd be working with. In the past he never really understood why others did this. It wasn't as if they had any control over which tech they worked with on any given night. But maybe it was a way of fortifying oneself beforehand against the predictably unpredictable behavior of a few coworkers.

Just when Tesfaye had thought he'd seen all of Muldoon's quirks, a new one would be revealed, even more disturbing than the last. While Tesfaye walked by a dry erase board in the ER hall, he saw that Muldoon had written, "Your x-ray tech today is Sean," with the capital "S" outlined like Superman's logo. Tesfaye laughed at that and admitted to himself that some things Muldoon did were actually pretty funny. Funny, yeah, Tesfaye thought, but often over the line too.

Alone sitting at the computer, Tesfaye couldn't reconcile Muldoon's humor with his ignorance. When Tesfaye brought in his next patient, a nearly deaf elderly woman, he recalled a similar patient that Muldoon ridiculed by making his voice sound like the witch from *The Wizard of Oz*. That situation made Tesfaye really uncomfortable; he hoped he never heard Muldoon do that again. But it was Muldoon's rough handling of patients, probably born of some kind of frustration or lack of empathy, which bothered Tesfaye the most.

Later, he saw Muldoon ignore a patient's request for pain medication before her hip x-rays. When Tesfaye was about to ask her nurse about it, Muldoon told him it didn't matter, that he would be done with her x-rays in a few minutes anyway. Tesfaye had just enough experience to realize that hip x-rays go a lot more smoothly if the patient has had pain medication. Moreover, he knew that pain treatment was a patient's right if deemed appropriate by the doctor. When the woman screamed as they transferred her to the x-ray table, Tesfaye blamed himself for not being more insistent about the pain meds. It seemed that every time Tesfaye told Muldoon to slow down or take it easy, it had no effect.

On the third x-ray of the lady's hip series, Muldoon forced the woman to bend her knee and rotate her leg outwards.

"AAAHH! Stop!" the woman screamed in pain.

"Just one more picture! You're not helping me any. You gotta work with me here!" Muldoon admonished her.

Hearing this, Tesfaye lifted his head from the control panel and could almost imagine a crunching sound coming from the patient's upper femur. More likely out of laziness rather than ignorance, Muldoon had not followed protocol for a trauma hip series. That would have involved an x-ray that took a few minutes longer. Tesfaye was speechless but he figured it was too late anyway. After that third x-ray was digitized, Tesfaye saw what he suspected on the radiography monitor; the patient's hip fracture was displaced, with a sharp section of the femoral neck pointing sideways. But Tesfaye couldn't really prove that Muldoon had displaced it, he only knew that within the next day or two, a surgeon would struggle to align the sections of her fractured femur.

For much of the rest of the night, Tesfaye dodged being seen with Muldoon in the ER hallways; he didn't want to be associated with such antics. But Sean Muldoon's behavior was no secret in the Radiology Department, so Tesfaye doubted that if he told their boss about it, that anything would be done. Still, Tesfaye considered talking to her about it anyway. How Muldoon ever got into health care he had no idea. To top it off, Tesfaye had to hear his bigoted diatribe on Muslims, and how according to him, they shouldn't be in this country after the World Trade Center attacks. After a while, Tesfaye did everything he could to block out Sean Muldoon from his mind.

In two days the fall semester was starting, so between cases Tesfaye went over his new schedule. People like Sean Muldoon, he thought; give me a good reason to stay in college. It wasn't so much that Tesfaye didn't like x-ray, although the pressure in the ER was incredible at times. It was more that in the field of Geography, he saw a respected profession and a subject he always wanted to pursue. Plus, he envisioned that as he got older, it would be a good idea to work in a less physically demanding occupation.

With Muldoon out of the room, Tesfaye's mind wandered as his pen filled in the holes of all the zeros, sixes and nines on his pocket calendar. He was firm in his belief that now was the best time to go after this goal, before a wife, children and a mortgage.

But there was something deeper Tesfaye was beginning to feel after working as a tech for three years. Although he handled the frequent stressful situations in a peaceful and calm manner, he wanted a light at the end of the tunnel. Since coming to America, and more so as an x-ray tech, Tesfaye learned that you had to work hard for everything here. And everything costs so much here. In Africa, so many people have no jobs that if you do have one you can live pretty well. Also, over there, though good jobs are few, they often have the security of being a job for life. Tesfaye had a hard time comparing the two cultures in relation to work. Ultimately for him and for now, it was all about opportunity.

Chapter 5

Tesfaye had spent Monday sleeping late and then picking up a few items for the fall semester. On Monday night, he went to Ivan Denovich's apartment to play chess and have a few drinks. Ivan worked exclusively in CT, also referred to as CAT scan. Other employees, like Sean Muldoon, Ron Koharski and Tesfaye were in a rotation that took them into CT on a less frequent basis.

On Tuesday morning Tesfaye had his first class, Soil Composition and Conservation. "It's a dirty job but someone's got to do it," was just one of the corny jokes the professor dished out in attempts to entertain his group of yawning twenty-somethings. Their next class promised to be more adventuresome, the instructor claimed. They were to meet along the banks of a nearby creek to see "real mud in the wild," as his teacher had put it.

With work and school, Tesfaye hadn't had the chance to be

outdoors much lately. He missed that and often thought about his childhood outdoor adventures in Africa. One memory of Ethiopia got triggered when Tesfaye saw a bicyclist on a hill outside Rochester. When he was ten or eleven, Tesfaye borrowed a friend's bike for a ride. He ascended a modest hill, passed over the top and gained speed. Men and women began screaming at him to stop, but Tesfaye had lost control. "Rat-a-tat-a-tat" was the repetitive sound his wheels made as they ran over the people's grain crops laid out to dry on the side of the road. They angrily chased after him, yelling for him to stop. But that, of course, was the last thing a ten year old was about to do. When he returned the bike, he reported to his friend only that the bike needed brakes.

Several hours after his morning soil class, Tesfaye sat in the breakroom at work eating dinner with coworker Megan McDonnell. Younger than Tesfaye, Megan had just completed her Associate's Degree in Radiologic Technology. A little tough on the outside, she grew up on the streets around the hospital.

"How's your sub?" asked Tesfaye about Megan's sandwich.

"Okay. What, no sheep's intestines for you today, Tes?" Megan wasn't about to let Tesfaye forget the time he brought in an Ethiopian favorite.

Tesfaye laughed. "No, not today. But actually it's really good. You should try it sometime. It's not as chewy as the stomach."

"Enough, too much information. It's bad enough I had to wipe my off my shoes after that last patient. Now you're grossing me out while I'm eating."

"Well, you brought it up, not me."

"Hey, isn't school starting this week?" Megan asked, quickly changing the subject and then taking a huge bite of her sub. The amount she ate for someone so thin really surprised Tesfaye. He attributed it to her young age, abundant energy and frequent exercising.

"Yeah, I had my first class today." He gave a brief

description of the classes he was taking. *Obviously,* Tesfaye thought, *she's not interested in this.* In fact, she was flipping through a magazine pictorial on celebrity plastic surgeries. Tesfaye understood that talk of map making and geography studies couldn't compete with botox and breast enlargements. Tesfaye took a bite of his extra hot chicken wings while Megan talked.

"Oh, I got to tell you. When Sean Muldoon came into work last night, he kept complaining that Melissa dumped him. He was so heartbroken. He was pathetic. I told him, Melissa is a friend of mine and he should watch what he says. I told him that she's too good for him anyway. I think he makes her sick. I mean she was in the ER again the other day with stomach pain. He's such a jerk. I hope he leaves her alone," said Megan.

"The other night, I worked with him. He was acting really strange. You know, kind of crazy. The things he says to patients. The way he handles them. I mean, he's really rough," said Tesfaye cautiously.

"Did you report him? You know you should tell Gilbert." Ellen Gilbert was the rambling radiology manager at All Saints.

"No, but I will. But, you know, he keeps getting in trouble and she does nothing about it. Like that argument he had with Dr. Goldman right in the middle of a spine surgery."

"I know what you're sayin'. A few weeks ago, Muldoon comes into the control room and takes out a handful of metropasses that he got from somewhere. I think they were the monthly ones that you can use on the bus and subway. Well, a couple of people wanted to buy one – and listen – Ellen was one of them. I heard her ask him to stop by her office, that she would buy one for her brother." Tesfaye tried to respond but Megan was on a roll now. "You know, sometimes I wonder if they're related. And then there's his constant sexual harassment and gross talk about his bodily functions. Enough already!"

Guessing that she was finished, Tesfaye spoke. "Yeah, you know what bothers me the most though? It's how he treats the patients. The ones that can't complain to the nurses. You know, they're senile or something." Seeing that Megan had her mouth full, Tesfaye continued. "It reminds me of a story my grandma told me once. You know, when I was a little kid. It's supposed to be a very old Ethiopian story." Tesfaye waited a moment to see if he still had her attention and then started up again. "There was this leopard cub. He got lost, I mean, you know, he wandered away from his home. He didn't know he was in danger. So, the elephants, they step on him, killing him. Another leopard finds the body and goes to tell the cub's father. The father leopard is so upset and angry. Well, basically, you know what happened? The father leopard, that's Sean Muldoon, he says that he doesn't believe it was the elephants. He denies it. So, he says, 'It's not the elephants who have killed my son. It is the goats. Yes, it must be the goats!' Then the father leopard, he searches and he finds a herd of goats and kills them all."

Megan finishes swallowing, takes a drink and asks, "So, I think I get it. Muldoon is the father leopard and the patients are the goats. But what are we?"

"I don't know," said Tesfaye. "My grandmother never told me that part."

Chapter 6

Megan McDonnell had window fans running in three rooms of her father's house. It didn't help. She did everything she could to make her father comfortable. Meg promised herself she would someday have a house with central air. Her father called out to her as she brought him his lunch.

"Meg, could I have some ginger ale?"

"Okay, dad."

Once in the kitchen, she got a glass from the cabinets next to the back window. Through that window, her eyes took in their small city yard and the pool that hadn't been used since her mom passed away. Those childhood years with mom went by so fast, she thought.

Meg's mother had worked down the street in the laundry at All Saints Hospital for thirty-two years. Her mother and father raised two girls. Meg and her older sister Kathy, both now worked at All Saints. Meg worked in x-ray and Kathy, married with three children, worked in respiratory therapy. Their mother bore the brunt of the labor through their childhoods. Their father lost his job at Rockwell Steel twenty-one years ago and hadn't worked steadily since. Meg was only two years old then. Carrying the meal to her dad, she glanced at the grandfather clock. Two-fifteen. That would give her enough time to go rollerblading before meeting her friend at the mall.

In her bedroom, Meg changed into workout clothes and pulled her rollerblades out of the closet. She said goodbye to her dad, grabbed her MP3 player and went out on the front porch. Sitting on the front steps, she strapped on her rollerblades, feeling the sun beat down on her shoulders through her short turquoise t-shirt. She vowed to stay in the shade as much as possible, fearing a burn on her fair skin. Making her own breeze was her immediate goal as she accelerated down the street toward Sycamore Park, her shoulder-length feathery blonde hair flowing behind. At the intersection, Meg passed little Sinclair College on her left with All Saints Hospital looming just behind it. With fortuitous timing, Meg shot across Greene Street, turned right and then left a half block down to enter the park. She leaned forward to get the momentum needed to go up a long incline, dodging kids and dogs by an old, yet currently functioning, fountain.

Coming up was her favorite part, the part that made all the expended energy worthwhile. Cresting over the hill, Meg's line of sight opened up, giving her a panoramic view of the vast green grass of baseball diamonds and soccer fields. Her sweat's evaporation cooled her. In a moment she was weaving through tall trees, enjoying the play of light through their canopy onto the path. Eventually, feeling totally invigorated, Meg slowed and stopped for a drink at a water fountain. In her pleasure, she had totally forgotten the frustrations she felt as a new x-ray tech at All Saints Hospital.

It seemed like so much of what she learned in her first two months on the job, she had learned the hard way. Like how to deal with a demanding surgeon, a patient that asks too many questions or a coworker's sexual harassment. For the time being though, Meg forgot about these things as she took another sip of water. She even forgot momentarily that she had to work at eleven that night.

3:00 p.m.

The sweltering heat outside meant that air conditioners inside could barely keep up. Second shift that day started out like any other for Tesfaye. When he clocked in at three p.m., he felt relieved to be in the relative coolness of the hospital, even if it was to work in the Emergency Department.

At three forty-five p.m., the ER secretary heard the first call on the ambulance radio. An explosion in the filled auditorium of Sinclair College, practically adjacent to All Saints, had knocked out a wall. When it happened, the secretary and others in the nurses' station felt the percussion and heard the blast. There could be dozens of casualties. Sirens whined and a cloud of gray smoke drifted skyward. Police, fire and ambulance squads arrived on the scene. But the close proximity of the disaster to All Saints enabled the EMTs to immediately begin wheeling patients, mostly students, into the ER. In addition, groups of ambulatory patients flowed into the waiting room. At this point, the most emergent patients gasped with short breaths approaching respiratory failure.

Kathy Martin, Meg's sister, stopped Tesfaye in the hall outside the X-ray room. She pulled her short black hair around her ear and cupped her nose and mouth for a moment. The oily smell from the explosion had made it into the hospital. Kathy told Tesfaye to get ready for a bad night. Kathy said she expected to be giving breathing treatments for smoke inhalation her entire shift.

When Tesfaye told Ron Koharski, the other x-ray tech assigned to the ER, what Kathy said, Ron blew it off. He claimed that even after the World Trade Center collapsed there weren't that many that needed x-rays. According to Koharski, the techs at hospitals across Manhattan had geared up for an event that unfortunately had more deaths than injuries requiring x-rays. Then Koharski ventured in the direction of the nurses' station, saw the patients on stretchers lining the hallway with EMTs and paramedics waiting with them, and thought Kathy could be right.

Up and down the pastel colored corridors of the ER, coughing and complaining could be heard mixed in with overhead pages. Initially, Koharski and Tesfaye did several portable chest x-rays at bedside for shortness of breath. No problem, thought Ron Koharski, wearing a desert camouflage scrub top. He carried x-ray cassettes back to be digitized in the x-ray room. Tesfaye continued on with the portable machine.

On one such chest x-ray in the crowded corridor, Tesfaye slipped an x-ray cassette behind a gasping barrel-chested nursing student. He put a lead apron on her to shield her abdomen from the radiation.

"Do you have a history of asthma?" Tesfaye asked after seeing the shape of her ribcage. Tesfaye pushed away a janitor's pail to make room for the oven-sized portable machine.

"Yes, and allergies too," she said, her voice muffled by the oxygen mask.

"Excuse me, sir! Excuse me!" A middle-aged woman tapped on Tesfaye's shoulder before he could shoot the x-ray. He aligned the beam with the patient's lungs.

"Excuse me. I need help! My mother rang for the aide twenty minutes ago. This place is a madhouse. I'm never bringing her here again. You know the nursing home sent—"

"—I'm sorry. Will you please step back? I'm shooting an x-ray here. I'll talk to you in a minute," interrupted Tesfaye. He told the student to take in a deep breath before he pressed the exposure button. Tesfaye maneuvered the machine around her stretcher. The middle-aged woman had found a nurse among a group of visitors waiting to find out where their family members were.

Tesfaye was stopped twice more by patients or family before he made it back to the ER x-ray room. He nearly tripped over two girls sitting side by side along the wall. An orthopedic surgeon told him he'd soon need x-rays done on a little boy. A dusty firefighter with a bandaged hand sat in a wheelchair outside the x-ray room door. When Tesfaye stepped through that door and into the dim light, he heard the robotic buzzing sounds of the refrigerator-sized digitizer and saw its flashing green lights. Koharski fed exposed cassettes into the machine.

"This reminds of a night a few years back when a train derailed and there was a chemical spill. We had a ton of chest x-rays that night too," said Koharski. Ron Koharski saw himself as able to handle anything the ER could dish out. He boasted that he was the "number one tech" at A.S.H., even jumping outside his job duties to take a turn at CPR chest compressions when an EMT needed a break. Anyone working in the ER knew when he was around; his loud raspy voice was unmistakable. A true veteran of ER wars, he'd fought through ten years of pulling double shifts in "the pit," as some referred to the ER x-ray room. But the years had taken their toll. Tesfaye saw him as an aging soldier, a guy who should have been a drill sergeant but somehow ending up taking care of patients. Still they worked together well. Tesfaye decided to basically go with the flow of his more experienced coworker. Sometimes Tesfaye would notice Koharski was limping. Megan had heard that he played a year of college football until he wrecked his knee and dropped out. Others guessed that he used to take steroids to bulk himself up. The truth was that he spun out his motorcycle on a highway outside of Daytona Beach while in college. He had been hospitalized in critical condition for a week after having reconstructive knee surgery.

Koharski had a reputation for working hard and playing hard, but his best days of both were over. Often he complained of extreme sports injuries such as the time he flipped over his snowmobile and it landed upside-down on top of him. He had three broken ribs from that and he made sure everyone knew about it.

Together, Tesfaye and Koharski kept up with the x-rays requested after the explosion. The ER charge nurse guessed that there would be no more than thirty to forty victims coming into to All Saints. She told Tesfaye this, and he considered it an underestimate because there were already thirty-five ambulatory patients in the waiting room plus a dozen on stretchers in the hallways. The nurses didn't seem too concerned as Tesfaye saw them heading out in pairs to smoke at the ambulance bays and check on the EMTs bringing in the patients. They knew the ambulances were taking several students to other emergency rooms across the city. Outside by the ambulance bays, television crews set up cameras for news reports. They shot video of the debris that was once a wall at Sinclair College. They zoomed in on paramedics giving oxygen in the parking lot to coughing students. And they followed nurses and EMTs pushing stretchers across the asphalt.

At four forty-five, Ellen Gilbert, the radiology manager, phoned Koharski in the ER to see how they were managing in the aftermath.

"Everything's under control here. We've done mostly just chest x-rays so far."

"Listen Ron, there's something else. I just got calls from St. Paul's and from the county hospital. Their power is out. Some kind of brownout from all the air conditioning on the power grid. They don't know how long it will last but they've put their ERs on divert status. You're bound to be affected by this later tonight."

"That really sucks. You know Ellen, we wouldn't be in this situation if the state hadn't closed three hospitals."

A statewide hospital restructuring commission had, two months earlier, enforced its mandate to close hospitals in the Buffalo area. By eliminating a glut of unused hospital beds, the state theorized that it would save millions.

"We'll just keep plugging away here. Tesfaye and I can handle it," Koharski claimed.

"I'm leaving in a few minutes, but if you want, I think I can get Megan McDonnell to come in early," said Gilbert.

"All right, whatever you think. Thanks, Ellen," Koharski said, hanging up the phone. At that moment, the lights and the computer screens flickered off then back on. The air conditioning unit also shut off for a few seconds then roared on again. A variety of beeps and hums came from the computers and the CR (computed radiography) equipment as they booted themselves back up.

Koharski called out to Tesfaye, who was busy positioning a young woman for a facial bone x-ray, "Tesfaye, did you see that. We might be next to lose power!"

"Ah well, you can't shoot x-rays without power," replied Tesfaye.

"You got a point there."

Tesfaye's patient complained of pain in her ankle, lower back and hip. She asked him if he could x-ray those spots too.

"At this point, I am only permitted to do what the doctor ordered," he explained, noting that the woman walked fine, in spite of the lacerations to her face from building fragments in the explosion. He asked her to lift her chin against the vertical x-ray board, getting ready to shoot an x-ray known as the "Waters," it could demonstrate bleeding into the maxillary sinuses.

Koharski stood by the CR workstation and swore. "Tell me what were they thinkin' when they closed those other ERs," he said to no one in particular. "Now I have to wait for the CR to reboot, and the digitizer to go through its self-test. Tesfaye, take her outa here. We'll label her cassettes and process them when the system comes back up. Meanwhile let's get the another patient in here."

Next, Koharski went back to the nurses' station to check where other patients were located. Only a curly haired secretary remained to answer the phone in the now deserted station. Every staff member was busy with a patient. Ron Koharski walked to the completely filled patient board, swore, and rubbed the stubble on the back of his shaved head. A few minutes earlier the dry erase board was half empty.

In the hall, eight new patients lay on stretchers. This time there was one major difference. All eight were strapped to backboards with cervical collars on. That usually meant work for x-ray. One of them, apparently pregnant, was yelling, "It hurts! I told you to stop." Her nurse tried to pacify her while drawing her blood.

Tesfaye pushed a patient by Koharski. He told Koharski the story. All eight new patients were struck by a portion of the ceiling that fell on their heads. Though they didn't seem badly hurt, the ER physician informed Tesfaye he would be ordering cervical spine studies on each. Tesfaye took it in stride; he believed he could weather this storm if he just stuck to the basics by doing one at a time. He trusted the ER physician, Dr. Mughari, to decide who should come first if there was any question. Koharski thought otherwise, he instructed Tesfaye to do each case in the order that the requisition was received and to change every order to a limited two view study. Tesfaye agreed only because the ER x-ray room was Koharski's show as long as he was there. Trying to do anything else would be like paddling up the Niagara River rapids in a canoe.

Tesfaye explained to the first of the cervical spine patients that he would be taking a couple of x-rays of his neck to see if the doctor would give the go ahead to remove his c-collar. Koharski came in, counted the growing stack of eighteen x-ray requisitions, and began complaining that he had told Gilbert three years ago that a second ER x-ray room was necessary.

"This proves my point. They build a brand new expanded ER, spending millions, and they didn't give us another x-ray room. And another thing, our equipment is beat; it's got to be thirty years old! Every dime in the last couple years has gone into CT."

"But it's mainly the power failures that are causing our problems now. I think the same thing would happen with two x-ray rooms," Tesfaye countered.

Koharski threw all the previously shot x-rays onto the digitizer now that it was running again.

"I'll be in the hall doing some of these extremity x-rays with the portable machine," he told Tesfaye just as Megan walked in. With Koharski out of the room, Tesfaye's eyes met Megan's.

"Man, am I glad to see you." The night really began to wear on Tesfaye, especially since he had classes early that morning. He felt his back getting sore and tightness in his legs.

"Tes, you guys are getting killed down here. Your eyes are all pink. Did you tell Gilbert you needed more help?" Megan asked.

"That's why you're here, right? Thanks for comin' in. Ron is not dealing with this too well. You know how he gets," Tesfaye said.

"Yeah, I know, he's gotta run things his own way and blow off steam the whole time. But he's not the number one tech for no reason," Megan replied. Then she added, "Ivan and Muldoon are having a fit over in CT. They're running two scanners but the power keeps cutting out. They've had to restart the system four times and now they're really backed up. And of course, one of the transporters is missing in action."

"Let me guess: Willie Stiles. As far as the computers go, we've had similar problems over here, too."

"I'll start taking patients across to the main department. Kevin and Stephanie will come over to help soon. They're on their last surgery cases. And don't worry, we'll get through this," Megan promised.

"Does this look like a worried face to you?" Tesfaye asked with a phony smile. Megan was great to work with, he thought, as he watched her take a requisition and go out the door. For the brief instant before the door closed, Tesfaye heard loud crying coming from the adjacent room. Then came the banging of fists on

40

the shared wall and muffled yells of "No! No!" A shiver went down Tesfaye's spine as he realized the "grieving room" was filled with a distraught family. Later, he found out that one of the construction workers at Sinclair had been brought in D.O.A., and lie in a nearby room. Tesfaye tried to block it all out and turned back to his patient.

Confident that his cross-table cervical spine x-ray was quality work, Tesfaye took the patient out of the room without waiting to check the image. He immediately moved on to the next c-spine. Koharski came in with a stack of x-ray cassettes he had used for the "clinic" that he set up in the hallway.

"My knee is freakin' killin' me. I had each patient sitting on the floor to x-ray mostly feet and ankles. All that bending over – I must have done something to it," Koharski complained. Tesfaye heard Koharski, but he wasn't really listening. The young nursing student he prepared to x-ray was hysterical and wanted to get off the backboard.

"Take this collar off me, I'm okay, really I am. Please unstrap me, I need to use the bathroom!" she insisted.

"I have to x-ray your neck and check it with the doctor first," Tesfaye explained.

Koharski barged in, ripped off her cervical collar, took off her backboard straps and sat her up.

"There. You're freed," Koharski said.

"Thank you! Those friggin' terrorists blew up our school! I saw two of my friends get crushed. I knew this was going to happen. Last year, one of those Yemenis threatened to do something like this. She said she was gonna' sue the school for discrimination," exclaimed the student with bulging eyes.

"It was only a matter of time. Now get up. Tesfaye, take her x-ray standing at the board," said Koharski.

Having grown up peacefully with Muslims in Africa, Tesfaye didn't buy it. In Ethiopia, Christians and Muslims were for the most part friendly towards one another. Tesfaye was used to them. He accepted them. If it did turn out to be Yemenis, he thought, that would surprise him.

The young woman slowly got off the stretcher and took five steps to the x-ray board. Then she collapsed to the concrete floor without warning, knocking first into the wall with a thud. Koharski and Tesfaye crouched over her. Tesfaye turned her on back. She opened her eyes, moaned, saying she was okay.

"I don't know what happened," she admitted.

Tesfaye got her back on the stretcher, gave her a cool cloth and moved her stretcher into position for her neck x-ray. Koharski took off to get another patient. In the noisy, brightly lighted corridor, he nearly collided with Dr. Mughari. They both winced at a foul stench permeating the area.

"Mughari, what's goin' on here? Look at this patient's requisition: both hips, cervical and lumbar spines, both feet and ankles. You gotta' be kiddin' me! If you had one iota of clinical skill, you wouldn't be ordering all these x-rays," blasted Koharski.

"I did examine that patient. A ceiling joist fell across her neck and back. What would you do if you were the doctor and I was the x-ray tech? I bet you'd order even more exams!" retorted Mughari.

"But Mughari, if it wasn't for your Muslim 'friends' we wouldn't be in the middle of this in the first place."

"What is that supposed to mean?"

"Come on, you know as well as I, it was Yemenis that blew up Sinclair."

"That's not true. I just heard from a fireman that construction workers were searching for a gas leak when it happened. They were in a room next to the auditorium when the gas exploded."

"Believe what you want, Mughari," Koharski said as he walked away with a now noticeable limp. Rounding the corner, he narrowly dodged an EKG technician, two nurses and Willie Stiles, slowly pushing a patient and stretcher, on his way to CT.

Kevin Collins returned from the OR and came over to the ER to help. Koharski asked him, "Can you take this case to the main department?" Collins examined the requisition.

"All right. Wow, why don't we just x-ray her entire body?" Collins said facetiously. Taking the paperwork and the patient, Collins left the ER. Koharski sought the next patient. Megan brought in another one of the eight patients who had cervical collars on and started to return the one Tesfaye had just completed. Tesfaye imagined they would be busy all shift long. Everyone seemed to be pulling together and doing what he or she could.

"Meg, the ER secretary called, they want us to do the elbow next," Tesfaye said.

"I think Koharski's is doing that with the portable machine," Megan replied. In the midst of the explosion victims, patients with typical summer injuries continued to come in.

The little patience that Ron Koharski had for children eroded to nearly none when he attempted to place an x-ray cassette under six-year-old Miguel Rodriguez's arm. The child screamed. Heads turned. Koharski teased the boy, "Don't blame me if this hurts. I didn't make you go on the trampoline." He glared at the parents standing away from the scatter radiation.

Two hours had passed since Megan got called in. Now, Tesfaye and she were clicking well as a team. Once, when they got a call for two more STAT portable chests, Megan suggested they do the child's game, Rock, Paper, Scissors to see who would go. Tesfaye shrugged his shoulders.

"Rock, Paper, Scissors?" he asked. "What's that?"

Megan laughed, told him his education was incomplete and quickly explained the game. Koharski entered the room just as Tesfaye put out his "Paper" to cover Meg's "Rock."

"Ha! I win!" Tesfaye exclaimed.

Koharski snapped, "Great, I'm dealing with screamers and you two are in here are playin' games!"

They seemed to be getting caught up with the ER x-ray requests, but that wasn't the case over in CT, on the opposite end of the hospital. Sean Muldoon was fit to be tied. Nothing seemed easy for him tonight. Four times Muldoon blew IV lines using the pressure injector for pulmonary emboli studies. Frustrated with that and the electrical interruptions, Muldoon's attitude toward the ER went from comic sarcasm to open hostility.

Turning to Ivan, the other tech in CT, he said, "If those idiots would stop calling us every five minutes, maybe we could get some scans done. And where is that Willie Stiles? Gilbert should have fired the bum a long time ago! This is the second time he's disappeared tonight." Ivan Denovich just looked at Muldoon.

"Page him through the operator. Or go get a patient yourself," suggested Ivan.

"It'll be a cold day in hell before I start getting patients," replied Muldoon, opening his cell phone to call his ex-girlfriend.

By eight p.m., most of the x-rays for the explosion victims had been completed. It helped that so many patients had left without being seen, apparently tired of the wait and not seriously injured.

Kevin and Stephanie had returned to the OR for add-on cases related to the blast. Tesfaye got the grim news that four construction workers had been found dead and were now in ER rooms awaiting the next of kin and morticians. He made his way through the maze of patients along the walls on stretchers, now exacerbated by the arrival of their families. The ER charge nurse seemed to have done nothing to alleviate the congestion. Several students with minor injuries sat on the floor because no beds were available. The beeping of occluded IV lines and the doorbell-like sounds of dislodged monitor leads continued.

Tesfaye sought the little boy with the elbow injury. Dr. Richard Banes, an orthopedic surgeon unhappy with the quality of Koharski's x-rays, requested repeats.

"Can I help you with the cart?" Banes offered.

"That would be great, I never turn down help," Tesfaye answered.

As they weaved around the corner toward the ER x-ray room, the grave-looking parents followed. The little boy, frightened because of his previous encounter with Koharski, cradled his fractured elbow tightly against his chest.

Banes explained to both Tesfaye and the child, "I'm really sorry to put you guys through this. Really I am. But I need of couple of better x-rays. I'm going to help take the pictures."

Koharski continued his mini-x-ray clinic down the hall with the portable machine. Megan came out of the x-ray room and saw the little boy's arrival with Tesfaye and Banes.

Smiling at the boy she teased, "Doesn't Dr. Banes remind you of Big Bird? See how tall he is." Banes also had a nasal voice and apologetic demeanor like Bird Bird's. A crooked grin emerged from the doctor's face. The boy just nodded.

After the final x-ray was done, a projection to demonstrate the head of the radius, Dr. Banes thanked Tesfaye profusely. "I really appreciate it guys. Great x-rays. Thank you so much."

"You're welcome, Doctor. Anytime," Tesfaye replied. Turning to Megan who was completing the computer tracking, Tesfaye asked, "Meg, who is this Bick Burt?"

"What?"

"Bick Burt. You called Doctor Banes Bick Burt?" he said.

"Oh. You mean Big Bird! Tes, don't tell me you never heard of Big Bird."

"No, I never heard of him."

"He's a giant yellow bird on a kid's TV show. Sesame Street. Banes talks just like him."

"Ah, now I see what you mean," chuckled Tesfaye. "You learn something new every day."

"Stick with me kid and I'll teach you the really cool stuff in American culture."

Dr. Banes interrupted their laughter, coming back into the ER x-ray room.

"That other tech, uh, Ron, just fell outside your door," said Banes with concern.

On the floor, grimacing with pain lay Koharski.

"What happened?" Megan asked.

"It's my knee. Must have… I must have hyper-extended it again," he grumbled, holding the knee flexed with both hands. "Slipped on somethin', somethin' wet, reaching over a patient," moaned Koharski.

Tesfaye said, "Meg, can you get him an ice pack?" Then to Koharski, "Man, I think you're done for tonight."

"Naw, I just need a few minutes to recoup." Tesfaye got Koharski an office chair and wheeled him into the x-ray room, putting him at the computer.

"Stay put for a while. You can do the case tracking," Tesfaye said encouragingly. Megan gave him the ice pack.

"Good thing we're almost finished with the explosion victims," she said.

- o -

On the highway that runs along the Niagara River, a tour bus carrying a group of contented Chinese tourists sped southward at dusk. Max Johnson, the bus driver, always felt better when he escaped any tourist attraction, but especially one as busy as Niagara Falls in summer. Due to the intermittent power outages, a decision had been made by the tour guide to skip the Buffalo waterfront and continue to Chautauqua Lake.

Up ahead, the load shifted on a long flatbed truck causing one of the chains securing a ten-foot high coil of sheet steel to burst apart. The truck driver heard the popping links and immediately knew he was in trouble. Like a giant wheel the coil turned, then bounced off with a metallic crash and rolled away from the truck. The coil made a reverberating rattle as it headed down the highway.

Fifty yards behind, Max Johnson yelled as he swerved the tourist bus to the right to clear the giant coil. The flatbed truck up ahead of them had swerved too, because of its sudden change of weight distribution, and slowed to the right. Now stunned to see the flatbed on the highway shoulder directly in front of him, Max pulled the steering wheel hard to the left, veering around the flatbed. The bus skidded. Two left side tires blew out. Now Max lost control of the bus as its front dragged along the concrete median, throwing shards of the shattered windshield into his face. The leading right side wheels lifted as the bus spun around crashing broadside into the concrete. Passengers screamed as they were hurled atop one another into the aisle. With a loud scraping screech, the bus slowed to a stop, now facing the direction it came from. Max, lying unconscious over the steering wheel with his nose and seven ribs broken, had saved his passengers' lives.

Moans and shouts arose inside the bus cabin. Several people climbed out windows and ran to the side of the road. An eerie quiet set in at the scene, broken only by intermittent cries for help and traffic buzzing by on the opposite side of the median. Eventually, faint sirens and horns echoed from down the highway. When the fire trucks and ambulances converged, activity surged as rescue workers began pulling out victims. Two by two, the injured were sped away to the nearest emergency rooms.

Back in All Saints ER x-ray room, Kathy Martin had come in without being noticed. "I think you spoke too soon, Meg!" she said.

"Oh, Kathy. What do you mean?" asked Megan.

"The ambulance scanner just said that there's been a bus crash on the Thruway. Lots of injuries. Maybe fifty. Count on at least twenty or thirty coming here according to the charge nurse," warned Kathy.

Koharski cursed; his eyes had glassed over from the pain and swelling in his knee.

"I think we need to get organized, you know, we need to get ready for this," suggested Tesfaye.

"How about we ask the third shift tech to come in early. Who's on tonight?" asked Megan.

"Saam's on. But I don't know if she'll come in early with all those kids," Koharski said. Koharski pulled out his wallet, took two hydrocodone tablets from a small pocket. "Meg, will you get me some water?" he asked.

Megan returned with the cup and said, "I'll call Saam. Any other ideas?"

"You know what? I want to talk to the charge nurse and Dr. Mughari," answered Tesfaye.

Then out in the hall, Tesfaye explained his plan.

"Meg, this is what I think we should do. First, we get permission to use this linen room over here. We move the carts out. We set it up like another x-ray room. You know, with a portable unit. We'll put in a couple of tray tables with gloves, cassettes, sponges, tape and well, whatever we can think of to make it work."

"Sounds good, boss," replied Megan.

"One more thing," Tesfaye said. "I'm going to talk to Mughari. I'm going to ask him, in advance, if he can work more closely with us to let us know which patients to do first. I think we need better input from him, you know what I mean? Triage. Basically, that's what I'm talkin' about."

"Good thinking. I hope we get cooperation. I'll go try Saam," said Megan.

Finally, the usually ineffective charge nurse started to make efforts to clear the hallways. First, students with minor injuries were given discharge papers with unprecedented speed. This allowed dozens of family members to leave. Next, patients needing to stay the night for observation were admitted and sent to the floors. A few of the injured were sent to the OR holding room, awaiting debridement and surgical reduction of their open fractures. And some patients who hadn't yet been seen already had left, tired of the wait.

Tesfaye carried supplies to the now commandeered linen room. With realization that things were falling into place, Tesfaye felt confident he was doing everything he could. The power outage continued at St. Paul's and the county hospital. Evidently, that part of the electrical grid had sustained some kind of damage that wasn't yet determined. Strangely enough, the turmoil of the last few hours had ebbed into a quiet time. Almost too quiet, Tesfaye thought. During that calm, Koharski attempted to get up and walked a few steps towards the door. Meg and Tesfaye saw him, dragging his leg behind him.

"Man, you should go home. We'll be all right. Go home and get off that leg," urged Tesfaye.

"I'm not gonna' argue with you. Looks like you kids got everything under control here. I'm outa here," Koharski said, exiting before the end of his shift.

Megan took the lull as on opportunity to run up to the cafeteria to get some sandwiches. When she got back to the ER x-ray room, she thanked Saam who had just come in.

"Your choice. Ham or Tuna?" she asked Tesfaye.

"Ah, well, thanks," said Tesfaye, reluctantly reaching for the dried out tuna. "You know back in Ethiopia, we have a saying. It goes something like: if somebody gives you a goat, you don't look at its teeth."

"That's like what my mom used to say. You don't look a gift horse in the mouth," replied Megan with a laugh.

The procession of ambulance and rescue squad vehicles made their way through the streets towards All Saints. Like some kind of weird parade, they entered the ambulance bays and parking area behind the ER. Delivering their patients strapped to stretchers, the EMTs wheeled them along the hall to the nurses' station. The ambient noise level increased dramatically with doctors shouting out orders, nurses directing the EMTs to take the worst patients to rooms, and sirens still echoing into the corridor.

49

Tesfaye and Megan made last minute preparations. Saam had agreed to be set up in the converted linen room if necessary. Tesfaye reviewed the x-ray requests as they came in. He sorted them according to the most urgent, as best he could. After a brief discussion before the ambulances arrived, Dr. Mughari gave Tesfaye permission to determine which patients should come first. Mughari was to have the secretary call with any changes.

Sorting out the new requisitions, Tesfaye made three piles. One pile was for minor extremity work that could be done in the linen room. The second pile consisted of x-rays of larger body parts, such as abdomen and pelvis, which required the use of the x-ray table. The third pile contained what he considered the most life threatening, including possible heart attack and respiratory arrest. Most of this last pile turned out to be portable chest x-rays. To Tesfaye, bone x-rays were seldom as emergent as they might seem. One exception, he was aware of, was when a fracture was open. In that case, Tesfaye planned to expedite it, knowing that surgery would be imminent.

Megan began the first of what turned out to be seven portable chest x-rays. Fighting her way through the congestion of carts to make it to each bedside, Megan then enlisted the help of whomever she could, to get the cassette behind each patient's back. Meanwhile, Tesfaye brought Lin Lee, one of the bus accident victims, into the x-ray room. Saam retrieved Meg's exposed cassettes and began processing them. Pausing from her work, Saam assisted Tesfaye as they counted to three and slid the patient to the x-ray table.

Thank God that Chinese people tend to be small, she thought whimsically. Within the last couple weeks, Saam reached her patient weight record – she had the "opportunity" to x-ray a seven-hundred-fifty-pound woman admitted for gastric bypass surgery.

Tesfaye awkwardly communicated with Lee. She knew enough English that Tesfaye was able to determine where it hurt with the aid of pointing gestures. Probably a hip fracture, Tesfaye first guessed as Lee put her hand on her left groin. Could be the pelvis though, because her left foot is not turned out, he surmised. It took just one x-ray to prove it was the pelvis.

Together they set up for Lee's final x-ray, a side or lateral hip projection. With care, they lifted her other leg and rested it on a stool placed on the x-ray table. Lin Lee grimaced and moaned. Saam aligned the x-ray tube so that the beam would shoot horizontally through the groin from the opposite side of the table. They jogged behind the leaded glass partition and pressed the exposure button.

Within minutes they were reviewing their images on the monitor, relieved that they were diagnostically acceptable. Tesfaye never doubted for a minute that they would be.

Megan turned from her portable paperwork and congratulated Saam and Tesfaye. "Nice shot there, guys."

Then later, after Tesfaye got back from returning Lee to her room, Megan approached him at the x-ray room doorway. "The Wild Mouse, that's it, tonight's like the Wild Mouse. You know, the roller coaster at Adventure Kingdom?" Megan asked.

Tesfaye stared blankly at her. He thought, *if only she knew me better*.

"Don't tell me – you don't know what a roller coaster is?" she asked.

"No, no, no. It's just that I've never been on one," admitted Tesfaye. "I never had the chance to go since I came to America."

"Well, Tes, you and I will have to go sometime."

Tesfaye laughed, though he doubted that trip would ever happen. He thought she was really cute and enjoyed working with her, as much as one could like working in the ER, but Tesfaye didn't see it going beyond that. Besides the fact that they were worlds apart in interests and experiences, Tesfaye noticed the not-so-subtle looks they got from other employees when they sat in the cafeteria together. He didn't really care what they thought. It was just that it brought him around to the reality of the situation, that Meg and he were just friends. And at this point in his life, dating a *farenj*, Amharic slang for Caucasian, wouldn't be a popular idea with his close-knit family.

Tesfaye flipped through the x-ray requisitions. Saam had made great progress at knocking out the minor bonework with a portable machine in the linen room. She returned and evaluated the current stack with Tesfaye.

"Check this out," said Saam. "Max Johnson, nasal bones, right ribs, chest and left knee x-rays. It says here he was the bus driver."

"I'll go get him," offered Megan.

Max Johnson's nose had swelled to twice its size. Although he had regained consciousness, Max remained motionless on the cart, with his head elevated just enough so he wouldn't swallow blood. Small flecks of windshield glass covered his black hair and forehead. Any change of position brought piercing pain to the right side of his chest. Luckily, the CT scan of his head was negative and now he could have his x-rays. Megan and Tesfaye steered the cart into the room.

"So, you're the hero I've been hearing about," said Tesfaye.

"Hero? Me? Don't make me laugh. It hurts too much," said Max. "Say, maybe you'll tell me because nobody else will. How are the others from the crash? I mean are they going to be all right?"

Now focusing on lining up the x-ray tube with Max's nose, Tesfaye replied cautiously. "You know, I don't know about each patient. But I know everyone survived. That's why one patient told me you're a hero, that if you hadn't moved the bus so quickly the metal coil could have crushed everyone."

Chapter 7

Professor William Hornsby stood bolt upright in front of his Cartography students. Little did they know that he was ill prepared for today's lecture. In fact, Hornsby had just come up with his lesson "plan" fifteen minutes before class. Tesfaye sat in the second row in a class of thirty-nine students waiting for the professor to begin. He had his pocket calendar out on his desk, making notes for the next week.

"First, let me say this: Air conditioning should be considered one of mankind's greatest inventions. It's so much easier when you have a class that's comfortable and wide-awake," Hornsby began.

Wide-awake? Tesfaye wished he were wide-awake. After last night in the ER, he was groggy along with being stiff and sore. Tesfaye heard this teacher was an oddball, but he thought he better not rush to judgments.

"I have to apologize in advance for an error on my part. The textbook for this course is still being printed. So, instead of a textbook, we'll be using handouts. And, unfortunately, the handouts are not quite ready, so we'll start with an assignment based on current events," said Hornsby, walking towards his desk. A girl across from Tesfaye tipped her head and shrugged. Tesfaye took it to mean she was already bored.

Hornsby held up the morning paper and began reading the large front page headlines. From where Tesfaye sat, he had no trouble seeing the biggest one.

"Four Killed in Gas Explosion at College," read Hornsby from the paper.

"Heat Wave Causes Brownout Across Region."

"Tour Bus Crash Injures Dozens on Thruway."

"Each one of these headlines has several direct ramifications relating to the study of Cartography," said Hornsby walking up to the dry erase board. Tesfaye's curiosity was sparked. Where was he going with this, he thought.

"Let me start things off. Then I'll turn it over to you people."

"Gas Explosion. What type of gas? Where does it come from? Where is it distributed? Can it be overlayed with population density maps?" he said, jotting key words on the board. Then he turned out to the class, "You in the baseball cap — your name is?" asked Hornsby.

"Michael Bowman," the student replied, barely audible.

"Okay, Michael, 'Heat Wave Causes Brownout Across Region.' What might the ramifications be to a geographer studying this?"

After a moment of chin scratching, Michael spoke. "Well, heat waves could be mapped out based on temperature readings at specific times and places."

"Good. Anyone else?"

"Electrical usage at specific times can be compared to, uh, outdoor temperatures," answered Tesfaye.

"Great. So you see where I'm going with this," said Hornsby. Launching into a long impromptu lecture that spanned from traffic patterns to the proximity of the huge hydroelectric power plants of Niagara Falls, Hornsby ate up a large chunk of class time. Some students found this dull, but the majority was engaged in the discussions that lead to the assignment.

"For next week's class, you will each have prepared a twenty-page Power Point presentation. You will base it on one headline from today's paper. You will propose how map overlays would benefit the study of your chosen topic. Any questions? Okay, see you next week. And don't forget to familiarize yourselves with the geographic information systems software in the lab."

After making a few notes, Tesfaye got up from his seat. He shook out the kinks that had come over his joints. In a short while, he felt better. The stress from the night before had dissolved throughout the morning. As he walked back outside in the brilliant midday sunshine, he felt purified by it. Tesfaye realized that he was spending too much time indoors lately. Working in a windowless x-ray department didn't help, he thought. He promised himself to return for a visit to his father's house this weekend in Rochester. A family picnic at a park really seemed like a good idea right about now.

Chapter 8

Friday August 31st Lake Erie Shoreline - 10:00 a.m.

Ron Koharski wiped the windshield of his new black wide body Ford F350 pickup. Though his wife had just had their first child, this truck was his new baby. Towing the trailer with his two ATVs inside had been a breeze. He adjusted the brace on his sore knee and then glanced at his watch. Muldoon was due any minute for a morning of riding the four wheelers along trails in an old quarry along Lake Erie. The barren moon-like terrain was strewn with boulders and piles of rubble. As usual, Muldoon was the only one he could find to accompany him on short notice. So many of his buddies now had a wife and kids. But he wasn't going to let that stop him from enjoying his life.

He didn't know how he put up with Muldoon's antics. The

only thing that Muldoon could be relied on for was to sell the metropasses and DVDs that they had acquired. That, and Muldoon kept his cop buddies out of the picture. But, it seemed to Koharski that every time he put his trust in him, Muldoon fell through big time.

He remembered last winter when he let Muldoon borrow one of his snowmobiles. Muldoon didn't return it for a month, and only after Koharski threatened to come and take it back with the help of an aluminum baseball bat. Then there was the time Muldoon didn't show up when they were to work Thanksgiving together. Koharski couldn't find a replacement and probably shot over two hundred x-rays that evening. What made that holiday extra "special" for Koharski was leaving the ER in order to do an emergency swallowing study with the on-call radiologist. Of course, Koharski recalled, the radiologist was "thrilled" to come in on Thanksgiving Day to perform the exam. Predictably, the patient had a piece of turkey stuck in his esophagus, which he miraculously expelled along with a mouthful of barium onto Koharski's new shoes. At least the man was "cured," he remembered.

Koharski turned back to study the Lake Erie shoreline in the distance. A dozen towering wind turbines rotated slowly on the site of an abandoned steel plant. He dwelled on the fact that it would have been an excellent day for his boat. But after racing it in the river last weekend, the engine was burning oil and kicking out blue smoke.

Muldoon arrived in his father's red convertible on the dusty road. Koharski was already driving the first ATV off the trailer ramp.

"What's the matter, did you have to have your momma wash your underwear before you left? You know, I was about to take off without you, Seannie-boy."

Sean Muldoon walked up with his coffee cup and spat in the dirt. He looked up with a grin.

"I had to kick your momma out of my bed," joked Muldoon.

"Nice comeback, loser. Now let's get riding before it gets too hot."

The vehicles roared to life as they bisected the quarry bed. The sun's rays burned through the dust on the desolate landscape. The two men stopped their ATVs at the top of a hill. Koharski reached behind him and took out a rifle with a scope. He pointed it towards the black, white and gray marked Canada geese a hundred yards away on the rocky shore of Lake Erie.

The Office of Ellen Gilbert - 2:00 p.m.

Ellen Gilbert was not Tesfaye's favorite person in the world. Not that he thought about his boss much, it was just that she didn't impress him. She always looked like she just rolled out of bed. She wore the same brown business suit every day, with wrinkles on the back of her blazer and a sheen on her pants. And Ellen's "let's talk it out" management style could give an insomniac a case of narcolepsy. She seemed to be all talk and no action. She was famous for her one-line words of wisdom such as "the art of life is constant adjusting to circumstances." Ron Koharski would intentionally misquote her by adding "circumstances beyond our control."

Being a relatively new associate, as employees were now called, Tesfaye had had only a few interactions with her. Lately, however, they had grown more frequent, usually typical scheduling issues. When he checked his cell phone around noon, Tesfaye noticed that Gilbert had called him during his morning classes. He returned the call. She wanted him to come in for a meeting, saying that there were several items to cover. If Tesfaye were the paranoid type, he would have gotten nervous. But he agreed to come in, more curious than anything.

After arriving at the hospital later, Tesfaye sat and waited for Ellen Gilbert to finish a phone call. He read the headlines of yesterday's paper sitting at the corner of her cluttered desk. The larger headlines he knew about from class the day before. A smaller headline sparked an idea for his weekly assignment. "Emergency Rooms Flooded with Explosion, Crash Victims," it read. Tesfaye believed he could do a presentation that sought to correspond emergency room patients' home addresses with ER locations. Basically, it would show the locations of ERs relative to their client base in a mock form—not based on real statistics.

Ellen Gilbert twirled her hair compulsively with her index finger. Her nondescript hair color was somewhere on the continuum from brown to gray. Instead of a romantic term like "mahogany," it could be described more like the hue of "wet cement." Her narrow, pointed glasses, worn down her nose, added to her matronly appearance. When Gilbert finished her call, she opened with a few complaints.

"Tesfaye, it's been brought to my attention that the radiologists don't like the patient histories you enter on the computer. They say there's a lot of a misspelling in the medical terminology. Granted, you're not the only one they mentioned, but I wonder if it's because of your language problems. You know, some people say they have trouble understanding you."

"That could be true. My English is not real good." He paused, and feeling a little perturbed continued, "Do you have trouble understanding me?"

"No, not usually. But about these spelling errors, you must really be more careful."

Tesfaye promised nonchalantly that he would try harder. He hid his concern that some of his coworkers could be cruel.

"And, I got a good report about you. Megan told me you did a great job Wednesday night after the explosion. She said you handled things really well after Ron left. So, I want to thank you for that."

Tesfaye smiled awkwardly, wondering if that was all that she called him in for.

"There's one more thing I want to talk to you about before you go, really more of an opportunity. We need a tech to serve as a quality assurance instructor and I immediately thought of you.

And, I thought it would be a good chance for you to practice your English. As a quality assurance instructor you would, after attending a class, be a spokesperson for improving the radiographic images here at All Saints. You could speak with our radiologists to see what they want. You could also collect examples of poor images and offer suggestions. Then, you would present your findings at the monthly staff meetings. What do you think?"

Tesfaye actually felt this was a compliment. He saw it as a way of getting to know his coworkers and the doctors better. It could be a great experience for him.

"Thank you for your, uh, confidence in me," he said. "It sounds interesting but, you know, I also go to school so I don't have a lot of spare time."

"We should be able to arrange for you to be taken off your regular duties to prepare your presentations. By the way, I'm sorry you won't be getting extra pay but I can get you comp time, say two hours a week."

Well, he thought, *I can at least give it a try.* Tesfaye agreed to do it. Gilbert seemed relieved that she had found someone to do the task. She handed him a hefty manual.

"Go through this. And start examining images too. I suggest you begin with Artifact Awareness and prepare a presentation for the monthly staff meeting." Artifacts ranging from metal buttons to hair clips often decreased the diagnostic quality of an x-ray, sometimes necessitating a repeat.

"Ellen, there's something I'd like to talk to you about. I mean, I have to tell you about something that's been on my mind."

"What is it? That's what I'm here for."

"Sean Muldoon. He's too rough with patients. The other night he made, you know, he forced an old man to sit up when the guy wasn't able. The man begged Sean not to sit him up because he had a bad back. Then Muldoon did it anyway and the guy, he screamed. That's just one example."

"Hmmm. I've had other complaints similar to this. I've talked to Sean about it, and he's been disciplined. But, let me ask you this. Were there any witnesses?"

"You mean besides me?"

"Yes, aside from you," Gilbert responded.

"No, we were the only ones in the x-ray room."

"Then it's your word against his," claimed Gilbert. "And he'll deny it."

"There must be something that you can do," urged Tesfaye.

"Not until I get a complaint from a patient or another witness. Preferably, someone outside of x-ray. You know, that reminds of one of my favorite sayings: 'You are what you tolerate.' "

Tesfaye felt puzzled and just looked at Gilbert. He thought telling Ellen about the incident showed that he *didn't* tolerate Muldoon's cruelty.

"What I'm trying to say, Tesfaye, is that I want you to hang in there and continue to report anything you find unacceptable."

Tesfaye drove home that afternoon with two resolves. First, that he wouldn't forget today's conversation. And second, that his new job duty would be a great distraction from the things he found unjust.

Chapter 9

A large indoor waterfall and manmade river rapids cascaded through the new Seneca Buffalo Creek Casino. Built after an agreement was reached between the previous governor and the Seneca Indians, the elaborate gambling facility glittered in what appeared to be an oasis of urban renewal. Groups of people loitered on carved stone benches while other gamblers entered through the blue glass atrium.

Muldoon and Koharski, both wearing black shirts with thick gold chains, passed through the large lobby. Koharski pointed to a poster for *Body Magik*, from Life Learning, Incorporated.

"Let's go check it out," Koharski insisted.

"What, and see dead people after they were injected with plastic and positioned like hockey players?"

After offering to pay for Muldoon's ticket, Koharski led his friend, passing large plasma screen TVs, into the exhibition hall connected to the lobby. Though well attended, *Body Magik* didn't quite live up to its name, they thought. It seemed more like *Bodies-R-Us*. Still, they were drawn to the multi-colored posed corpses, each in a dramatic sports position. The reactions from tourists ranged from obvious horror to serious anatomical study. Muldoon and Koharski felt a special attraction to the skinless female tennis player, artificial eyes wide open, clad only in a headband and about to hit an overhand volley.

Created from donor bodies by Chinese anatomists under the direction of a German doctor named Eisenhut, each figure demonstrated individually colored muscles as well as cut-aways that showed body systems such as cardio-pulmonary and genito-urinary.

To their right stood an eccentric looking visitor, slightly hunched over with long gray hair covering half his face. He was dressed all in white, a thin white sweater and sport coat with white cotton pants. A middle-aged man, Rod Calabrey visited Buffalo occasionally to see an elderly artist uncle of his. His own roots weren't far away either. Calabrey's early years were spent in the picturesque town of Watkins Glen, New York, known for its auto racing. But Rod Calabrey was the antithesis of a race fan. In fact, he abhorred it. Movies were his thing back then; they consumed his every weekend. He was the first of his friends to get a VCR and used it to overcome his lack of popularity in high school. And while Calabrey's classmates viewed videos in the paneled basement of his parents' home, he sketched the more attractive females. These girls ate up the attention like spoiled four-year-olds at birthday parties. And his skills grew to match their vanity. Calabrey ingratiated himself with the girls; he surrounded himself with them through constant drawing. His attraction to their beauty wasn't physical. It wasn't lust. He didn't want them. Rod Calabrey wanted to be one of them, especially the most exquisite ones.

His talent and skill led to a scholarship to Parsons School of Design in New York City. Living in a dormitory that occupied four floors of a decrepit sixteen-story apartment building on Union Square West, Calabrey continued to find a niche with the best looking female art and fashion design students. During the day, Calabrey labored during his *Anatomy for Artists'* and other classes. At night, he leveraged the looks of his girl friends to get into Studio 54. A serious student with a dream of being a famous artist, the young Rod Calabrey avoided the acid, the coke and the Quaaludes popular with that crowd.

Then in the spring semester of his second year of college, his life hit the accelerator. He tagged along with girl friends to a party in the penthouse at the top of his apartment building. The owner of the penthouse, a flamboyant fashion designer, was known for his extravagant parties and celebrity guests including Mic Jagger and Madonna. Sexy female art students like Calabrey's friends were always welcome there. They could be found in the foyer or riding the elevators, dressed and ready to sneak in on most late Saturday nights.

The second time that Rod Calabrey got into one these celebrations; he brought a large newsprint pad and created a charcoal portrait of pop singer Grace Jones. She loved it, especially the way he captured her trademark sneer. But more importantly, Calabrey impressed a successful comic book artist at the party who needed an "inker," basically an eager young artist to work like a dog at outlining and then coloring his rough pencil drawings. But, it meant a summer job for Calabrey. And it meant never having to live in his little hometown ever again.

From behind the spotlighted female cadaver, Calabrey's eyes briefly met Muldoon's.

"Hey, Koharski. Look over there. It's Andy Warhol," joked Muldoon.

"Who?"

"You know, the guy that painted the Campbell soup cans," answered Muldoon.

"Yeah, right, maybe they brought him back from the dead just for this show," said Koharski.

Overhearing their comments, the smallish man lifted his head, stepped out from behind the posed corpse and swept the hair from his eyes.

"Be careful what you say about Mr. Warhol. You know, he was really a great man. A hero of mine, actually. And I lived across Union Square Park from him many years ago in Manhattan. But alas, I never met him. He was so reclusive by then. That was sooo many years ago; maybe before you boys were even born. By the way, quite an exhibit don't you think?" A few people trickled by.

Taken aback that this oddball was speaking to them, Koharski and Muldoon were stunned. After a moment Muldoon answered with an affected tone, "Well, good concepts, strong attention to detail."

"I agree," the older man started. "This Dr. Eisenhut is a true artist. I think he's done an inspiring job here. I'd love to meet him some day. Do you see the way he's distinguished the major muscle groups? Look at the contrasting colors he's chosen to portray the body systems. And the poses are fantastic."

"He sounds like one of the doctors we work with," Koharski said.

Rod Calabrey introduced himself as a New York City artist. Then, picking up on the doctor reference that Koharski made, Calabrey asked, "So what type of medical work are you engaged in?"

"We do CT scans and x-rays at a local hospital," replied Muldoon. Calabrey perked up. The subject turned to CT technology as Muldoon described how new color imaging software enabled the creation of realistic 3-D reconstructions of bones, heart, and brain.

Rod Calabrey's mind made creative connections to what he was hearing and how he could profit from it. In the inner circles of both the east coast and west coast wealthy, oversized art merged with medical technology was in hot demand. One artist/photographer ran a pen-sized optical scanning device over every square inch of an actress's body. With these colored scans, he laid out a map image of her skin, like some kind of unfolded polyhedron. The portrait netted the artist a half million dollars. Calabrey predicted that the cutting edge of this trend pushed toward more and more intimate creations. He wanted to get in on it now, to strike while the iron was hot. Offhand, he could think of at least twenty of his patrons that would likely jump at the chance to have a Calabrey CT portrait.

Rod Calabrey tried to focus on Muldoon's description of the technology, but was driven to distraction by an intense need to see the scan images immediately. While Muldoon explained the purposes of particular scans, Koharski remembered who this artist was. He was known as the creator of giant photo-realistic portraits. Calabrey asked several questions and then made a proposal. He wanted to visit the CT department and see its capabilities for himself. He said he needed reference material for a hospital mural in New Jersey. Claiming that color CT cut-aways might be perfect for the project, Calabrey promised that it would be a lucrative venture for them all. Koharski's eyes rested on the grotesque figure in front of him with its bulging maroon quadriceps. He considered Calabrey's request. Koharski and Muldoon stepped aside for a moment.

"What a queer eye," said Muldoon standing with hands on his hips. "What do you think, Ron?"

Ron Koharski watched two young black women in neon green tee shirts inspect a nearby male cadaver. One of the women squeezed the blue bicep of the underdressed quarterback and giggled.

Koharski shook his head at Muldoon. "I'm not sure about this. He's a strange ranger. Anyway, I don't know about bringing him into CT. What if somebody sees him?"

"Ron, it's easy. We'll just have him come in at like three in the morning. No one will ever know. I'll tell him to wear a lab coat or something. Judging by what the dude's wearing now, he probably has one in his closet."

When they returned, Calabrey was more intent than ever at seeing the new CT technology. He offered to pay for a sample scan of himself. Calabrey said it would be easy money for them that would add to their casino winnings. Koharski studied the artist for a moment and then glanced at Muldoon. There were no casino winnings to add to, only losses to recoup. Koharski threw out a figure of five thousand dollars per scan, and to his shock, Calabrey took the bait. This would be like shooting fish in a barrel, Koharski thought. A date was set. The time selected for maximum secrecy, third shift. Quick handshakes and phone numbers were exchanged. As the two technologists passed by the casino's cascading indoor river, Muldoon imitated the creepy artist's hunched over stance and arrogant voice. Koharski laughed at Muldoon while patting himself on the back for striking such a lucrative deal with Calabrey.

Chapter 10

September 2nd Lake Ontario Shoreline – 2:00 p.m.

In a park overlooking Lake Ontario, north of Rochester, a well-dressed group of picnickers had found a shady spot under a stand of horse-chestnut trees. The small children in this extended family chased a soccer ball on this glorious late summer afternoon. They had just left the Ethiopian Orthodox Christian Church and then stopped back home briefly to pick up food and charcoal for the picnic. The idyllic spot was selected carefully. Their initial choice became disrupted when two teenage boys chased a girl with a large water gun. This appeared to be an involuntary wet tee-shirt contest. A quiet, more relaxed affair than that, Tesfaye's family talked and laughed. They ate traditional foods of their homeland including *injera,* a pancake-like bread and

68

doro wot, a chicken stew.

The aroma of grilled steaks brought Tesfaye over toward his father and stepmother. He had driven seventy miles for this party and savored being amongst his family. His stepmother glowed with her orange dress against her coppery skin. She greeted Tesfaye with three kisses on his cheeks. Then she hurried to get more items for the grill. Alone with his father under the trees, Tesfaye scanned the horizon. His father flipped over steaks as they sizzled with a sudden flame. Then Tesfaye's dad pointed to the expansive ultramarine blue lake. In the distance, a few sailboats clustered here and there. In the foreground, cattails lined the water's edge.

"You know, Tes, it's like a postcard isn't it? Or maybe it looks like an escape route," his father joked in Amharic.

Tesfaye smiled. The subject turned to Tesfaye's university studies and how his hospital job was going.

"It's going okay. A little bit of chaos with that explosion and bus crash I told you about. Oh. My boss asked me to give a presentation on Quality in X-ray." If his father was proud of him, it wasn't obvious, but Tesfaye knew it just the same.

His stepmother, now with an aunt, returned with more steaks to grill.

"You're not going to cook all this good beef, I hope?" Tesfaye asked. "Save some for me."

Fresh raw beef was a delicacy to many Ethiopians. Usually saved for special occasions, the beef would be sliced into small chunks and dipped into a mixture of hot pepper, other spices, and alcohol.

Also in Amharic, his aunt teased Tesfaye. "There's a pretty girl I know of back home who would love to meet you." Tesfaye laughed, and then deflected the attention by picking up his little sister running by.

"*Malkam ledat.*" Tesfaye held her close and wished her a happy birthday.

He wasn't sure about arranged introductions through family. Though they were common in Ethiopian culture, Tesfaye felt it was too soon for him to be thinking about it.

Chapter 11

Dominating the T-shaped ground floor of All Saints Hospital was the refurbished main lobby with its stained glass entrance at the T's top and center. This entrance was locked at eight p.m. After that time one could only exit from that point. Outside, Rod Calabrey walked by the main entrance and continued along the front of the building. Once he reached the hospital's far end, he turned the corner and sought an alley that Koharski had described. It was essentially trapped space created by the long MRI unit trailer parked next to the radiology department.

71

Though he had explicit directions from Koharski, in the night's darkness, Calabrey became perplexed. The presence of other trailers for construction confused him. He couldn't quite find the alley he was supposed to meet Koharski at. Discouraged, he thought perhaps he was expecting too much from tonight. He asked himself how he could ever have trusted these baboons.

Yet the clandestine nature of tonight's test scan invigorated him like a double espresso. Just then he heard a whistle, apparently coming from a space he had rejected as too narrow. From the shadows came Koharski in green scrubs, to retrieve the artist. Quickly, they entered the alley and proceeded to a propped open emergency exit door. Cigarette butts and coffee cups littered the ground. Carefully and with anticipation, Calabrey stepped into the harsh fluorescence of a radiology corridor.

At this hour, Koharski and Muldoon were the only ones working on this side of the hospital's first floor. Koharski rushed Calabrey into a hall outside the CT room. Koharski opened the heavy CT control room door. The darkened room glowed with several flat panel computer monitors, some with information, some with body imagery and one with the Internet. To Calabrey, the place was like some sort of subterranean command center, like a secret high-tech hide-away that the Pentagon would use in case of a nuclear attack. He wondered how an old neighborhood hospital like this could afford state-of-the-art medical equipment and computers.

Workstations at either end faced bright scanner rooms behind thick glass. Muldoon's wide back filled the padded chair at one workstation. He shot a backwards glance at the two arrivals, then peered through the large glass wall that separated him from the scanner and the patient within it.

The smooth modern contours of the seven-foot high scanner gantry contrasted the boxy wall cabinets, carts and monitors. Calabrey waited quietly for Muldoon to complete the exam so that they could speak openly. Muldoon pecked away at the keyboard and clicked on the computer mouse repeatedly. The scanner table hummed as it took the patient into the circular opening.

Within the scanner, the high-speed rotating x-ray tube gently buzzed radiation through the patient's skull. Slices of what appeared to be a brain showed up one by one on the monitor. Calabrey recalled once having a CT scan of his head years ago, but he certainly didn't see it from this vantage point. Now, he was thrilled and his pulse quickened. His mind extrapolated on the technology's creative possibilities with the human form. Calabrey imagined it might be possible to put two people in the scanner together. He wondered which composition would be best, superimposed figures or side by side.

In just minutes the scan was completed, then Muldoon reappeared after pushing the patient into the hall. Though wearing a lab coat with false ID, Calabrey was nervous about being seen by the transporter who had come to whisk away the trauma patient. After securing the doors quickly, Muldoon brought up a frontal image of a male torso on his computer. Calabrey and Koharski came closer.

"Welcome to the cash cow of the radiology department, Mr. Calabree," Muldoon wisecracked, mocking his name pronunciation. With eyes still transfixed at the computer's translucent torso, he corrected Muldoon.

"It's Calabrey, not Calabree, Mr. Muldoon. And can we please get on with the show now, if you don't mind."

A tense pause was interrupted when Koharski began, "What you see on this monitor is a topogram, basically a frontal projection of the body. It's not what you typically think of for a CT. It is not the slice of bread type of scan; it's the image that shows the location of the individual slices."

"It's marvelous. I can see everything. Wonderful. The ribs, the pelvis and are those skin creases? You can even see their clothing," Calabrey continued theatrically. The resolution on the monitor surpassed Calabrey's dreams.

"Mr. Calabrey. . ." Koharski said, ". . . there is a slight hitch, something to be worked out. The table movement limits the length of the scan. So if we start a topogram at the top of the head it would end somewhere down the lower leg." Rod Calabrey reflected on this for a moment, sweeping the hair from his eyes.

"But that is not my concept. As I previously explained to you, my concept is to do a full-length translucent portrait of an individual from head to toe. I want them posed with piercings, jewelry, clothing, accessories and the like. Why didn't you tell me this sooner? I wouldn't have come here tonight if you couldn't do the entire body." The artist seemed deflated.

Koharski replied, "We could of course do two scans, one for the upper section of the body and one for the lower. And, since you're going to digitally color them anyway, you should be able to manipulate the images on your computer to join them."

Calabrey thought about this for a moment. "Well, that sounds better. Could we do a scan now? Perhaps we could try one now?"

"Well, Calabrey, if you don't mind being the guinea pig," Muldoon replied. Not liking Muldoon's choice of words, Koharski shot him a dirty look. Then, instead of selecting from the computer list of "registered patients," Koharski chose "emergency scan," allowing him to set the parameters for Rod Calabrey's CT scan.

The narrow table onto which Calabrey laid moved surprisingly quickly with a humming sound through the open circle of the CT gantry. Though he had been assured that the radiation was very low, Calabrey believed he felt the beams penetrating his cells. At this point the phone rang. Koharski had to put off the emergency room secretary. They needed a scan done STAT of a car accident victim. Koharski realized this little presentation had gone on for too long. Thirty-five minutes had passed since the artist's arrival. Calabrey was so enthralled with his body scans that he spent precious time studying his own anatomy on the monitor.

Muldoon burned the scans onto a CD. Much to the disgust of Koharski, the artist didn't have cash and wrote out a personal check. Finally, Koharski erased the scans from the computer and directed Muldoon to escort Calabrey quickly out of the building.

Chapter 12

Actress Bethany Baird held her newly adopted Ethiopian daughter in her arms as she reached for her glass of chardonnay. She knew the infant should be back at the hotel with her nanny, but she couldn't bear to leave her, and this was a party she would not miss. Adorned with black pearls and wearing a golden gown with a wide enameled belt by Amsale Aberra, she was reminiscent of a Roman goddess from a 1940's Technicolor film. Even though she earned more than ninety million dollars in the last five years, Baird believed that her new movie's success at the Toronto International Film Festival marked her first real chance of an Oscar.

Over the shoulders of her companions—directors, producers and film executives—she spied Rod Calabrey and called out. "If it isn't my favorite artist! Rod, come over here."

Rod Calabrey brushed the long gray hair away from his eye. He lifted his head, raised his eyebrows and spoke. "So wonderful to see you again, my dear Bethany. And who do we have here?" Rod asked about the baby.

"Her name is Kayla and she's sound asleep. I'm trying to keep it that way. Anyway, you know how I love children. I brought her back from Africa. Isn't she perfect?"

Baird now had four children, including others from China, Vietnam, and Peru.

"Oh, yes, she's so precious. And *everyone* knows about Kayla. What a doll. Kayla's so lucky to have you for a mother. By the way, the film is marvelous, very surreal. It reminded me of a Salvatore Dali painting. And you were splendid." Again, Calabrey brushed his hair from his eye.

"Enough about me," Bethany said. "I loved your poster for the film festival. It's quite sensuous. I'm having one framed for my collection as we speak."

"You're too kind. It's really trivial, just a simple silhouette of two people romantically intertwined," remarked Calabrey. Event posters were usually beneath him. He did it only to have an "in" at the festival, to be amongst the Hollywood elite.

"Oh, but the way you imply the anatomy really is wild. And you did it without shading or linework." As a struggling young woman with aspirations to become an actress, Bethany Baird had modeled for life drawing classes at colleges in New York City. While the students reconstructed her contours, she developed her art lexicon. Around that time she met Rod Calabrey, a Manhattan based painter who went through models faster than a fashion magazine.

"Very perceptive of you, Madame. You know, speaking of anatomy, I have an idea that may interest you," Calabrey offered.

"Really? How intriguing!"

"Yes, I'm at the beginning of producing full length translucent portraits on glass utilizing the latest in helical CT scan technology."

"Wait. Wait. Wait a second. That sounds risky. I mean CAT scans use radiation, don't they?"

"It's completely safe unless you're pregnant," guessed Calabrey. The actress shook her head no.

"Anyway, it's no more risky than, say, flying in helicopters over the Horn of Africa, as someone I know is prone to doing."

"Probably not, but what would a CAT scan portrait of me be like?" Bethany asked.

"Oh, that's what I must tell you about. That's the best part. Incredible soft tissue details contrasted with your ribs, bones, and muscles. Your clothing superimposed. I'll take the full-length digital images and create layers of colors to be painted on large panes of frosted glass. And to further enhance the concept, I foresee ornamentation in the form of your choice of jewelry and accessories. Imagine such an image backlit, so that the colors glowed like stained glass. And think of the marketing potential for your product lines."

Bethany smiled broadly and in a moment they were having a toast, a toast to their new creative venture.

Chapter 13

The long drive back to Buffalo from Rochester gave Tesfaye time to think. It started with his aunt's comments the day before about having a girl she wanted him to meet. Tesfaye had heard it all before from well-intentioned, matchmaking female relatives. But this time it somehow stung like a bee.

As the miles clicked by on the odometer and with the setting sun in his eyes, Tesfaye dared for the first time to consider the ultimate blind date – an arranged introduction scenario.

In it, Tesfaye saw himself traveling back to the highlands of Ethiopia, reuniting with his mother, grandmother all his relatives again. Word had been spread of his desire to marry and photographs were exchanged. Relatives went to the homes of several young women of the nearby town to inquire if they were available and to seek parental consent.

Then comes the big day, the day when he meets his future wife hand-picked by the family. He sees her, a radiant young woman, a princess of Africa, also seeking a partner to share a life with—a life in America. In the daydream, they stand in a small but crowded church, Tesfaye wearing a white and gold tunic, his bride wearing a traditional white gown with a small crown. He marries her and they return to the U.S. to Buffalo, New York where he continues his schooling and work at All Saints Hospital. His bride studies to improve her English and gain a skill. Eventually they have children.

It was an easy scenario for Tesfaye to imagine. It didn't even make him the slightest bit nervous. But something didn't feel quite right about it. Having been in America for almost ten years, Tesfaye wanted a little more control over his life's direction. There was so much more to explore, more places to see, more people to meet and more of life to experience. All of this, he believed, would be so much more difficult with a wife and children. Yet, an aching loneliness that he had just begun to know in the last year slowly and almost imperceptibly crept into his consciousness. And added to that loneliness came an acute awareness that the likelihood of meeting a compatible woman in Buffalo were probably slim. However, back home in Ethiopia, he knew that he had assets that would attract many young women – a good job, education and American citizenship.

Time and distance had passed quickly while Tesfaye was engaged with his thoughts. As he approached the exit from the Thruway, he was surprised that he didn't remember much of the ride. Tesfaye found that stretch of highway from Rochester to be flat, unremarkable and hypnotic.

As he pulled into his parking spot at his apartment building, Tesfaye noticed the sky had darkened and the first stars were appearing. His imagined wedding in Ethiopia slipped back into his thoughts. Again, he evaluated it and wondered if American style dating would be better for him.

Tesfaye stopped in the hall and collected his mail from Saturday. As he separated the advertisements from the bills, he dismissed thoughts of marrying some woman he had yet to even meet. Anyway, there's no rush, he guessed, the girl might only be seventeen years old now.

After reheating some lentils and beef brought back in a care package from his father's house, Tesfaye settled down to eat it with some *injera* bread. He read a chapter in his Soil textbook for class the next day and made a few notes about the properties of clay, silt and sand.

An hour later, Tesfaye sat in Ivan Denovich's austere apartment for their weekly chess games. Tesfaye sipped a Bud, while Ivan poured himself a glass of raspberry vodka. Since both Ivan and Tesfaye had learned English as a second language, communication was sometimes awkward. Still, through chess and a few drinks, they managed to share some common interests.

Tesfaye had only learned chess since coming to America, whereas Ivan had played since he was five years old. Tesfaye skills and tactics had improved quickly however, with the help of a computer tutorial program. He also discovered earlier that summer that alcohol was a real detriment to playing chess. One mistake and the game would essentially be over. Tesfaye, therefore, let Ivan do most of the drinking. That seemed to even the playing field just a little.

While setting up the pieces, Ivan asked how things were going in x-ray. Tesfaye talked briefly about the explosion at Sinclair College and the chaos that night in the ER.

"Yes, I know these things. In CT, the power problems backed us up," said Ivan. Often, Tesfaye thought Ivan downplayed situations at work. He really wanted to talk about Muldoon's recklessness with patients, but couldn't bring himself to do it. Though Ivan was a dedicated and intelligent coworker, there was always something that stopped Tesfaye from being open with him. There was a certain aloofness Ivan possessed that Tesfaye attributed to cultural differences. Koharski said that Ivan reminded him of a Russian Sherlock Holmes—always watching with eagle eyes but only briefly sharing the inner workings of his mind. Tesfaye couldn't relate to this analogy. He didn't know anything about the fictional character.

Whenever anyone would complain about a fellow employee, Ivan fell silent, obviously reticent to join in any criticism. At most, Ivan would offer in his Russian accent, "But what you can do?" Tesfaye recognized that this type of reluctance could be a good quality, especially since the witch hunts and false rumors were all too common amongst hospital workers. Anyway, Tesfaye thought, now is not the time to talk about this and he considered his next move.

As the game progressed, Tesfaye and Ivan had protected their kings well, but Ivan controlled the board's center. One thing Tesfaye noticed was that Ivan always seemed to come up with a better move than the one Tesfaye guessed he would use. This constant evaluation of multiple possibilities made Ivan a great competitor. In contrast, Ivan didn't appear to be impressed with any of Tesfaye's moves. Tesfaye found this extremely frustrating, but then he began to look for better moves himself. He decided that each move represented essentially a totally new game not unlike how his life changed with each geographic change. Looking ahead in life, however, was another matter altogether for Tesfaye, consequences seemed hard to predict. Tesfaye's mind drifted back to how he had reported Muldoon to his boss, Gilbert, and now wondered if it was the right thing to do. She reacted as if she wasn't going to do a thing about it. Tesfaye began to consider that maybe because of this, he should go over Gilbert's head, and report it to her boss.

Again it was Tesfaye's move. Abruptly, he decided to try something Ivan wouldn't expect, something to catch him off-guard. Tesfaye attacked with his bishop, sacrificing it, and removed the pawn in front of Ivan's king. But Tesfaye had missed the obvious.

"You must be distracted by something," claimed Ivan as he took Tesfaye's queen.

"Ahhhh," moaned Tesfaye in shock. "Man, I saw your previous move, you know, when you threatened my queen, but somehow it slipped from my mind just before I made my move. I was doing so well up to then, too. I can't believe it, one bad move destroyed me." Tesfaye knew that loss of his queen generally meant a lost game against Ivan.

"You have to stay focused," Ivan said simply.

"It's a lot like x-ray, isn't it?" asked Tesfaye.

"What do you mean?"

"In x-ray and chess you have to believe that what you can't see is real. I mean the radiation in x-ray and the moves in chess," explained Tesfaye.

"But chess is only a game and radiation is real," replied Ivan with a smile.

Chapter 14

Tuesday September 4th Calumet Apartments

The long Labor Day weekend spent at his father's house was just the break Tesfaye needed. And his weekly chess match, though a losing effort, still held enjoyment for him.

Tesfaye felt that he was shifting gears now, just like most of the cars back home in Ethiopia, and heading up the hill of a new school year. For Tesfaye, that meant he would be working less at All Saints and more in the labs and classrooms on campus. Not a problem, thought Tesfaye, except for the fact that it still felt like summer.

In the morning, he met his classmates along the banks of a wooded stream near the university for a field technique exercise. Unfamiliar with the area, Tesfaye had a little trouble finding it, despite the geography teacher's map. After going down the same unpaved road twice and not seeing the stream, he finally called a classmate on his cell to get the final directions. When he got out of his car, Tesfaye squinted in the brightness and felt the warm sunshine on his face. He followed a path toward the stream between sumac trees, mostly green but with some drooping red leaves. Tall goldenrod bent in a light wind. He heard the other students by the water and felt lucky to be outside, instead of in the hospital.

Tesfaye and his classmates received their instructions. Each was to branch out and proceed to a pre-selected location. They would then dig to a depth of one foot and fill a small bucket with that soil. Each bucket was carefully marked to correspond to a map. While Tesfaye walked upstream and later when he was digging, he thought about how different it was than working in a hospital. Radiology was so far removed from the natural world that often it seemed like trees, streams, beaches and mountains only existed to enhance a vacation. And he considered that, for as lowly a substance as "soil" or "earth" was, no one can dispute that a basic understanding of it can be important to everyone from engineers to backyard gardeners. For now, that simple belief was enough to keep Tesfaye's mind on his studies.

Back home in the early afternoon, the window air conditioner in his apartment droned loudly. Lacking central air, his building was the standard two-story brick style built after World War II. The two-bedroom apartment was kept neat, decorated with African art as well as a charcoal portrait of Tesfaye done by a street artist in Manhattan. It was a good resemblance, Tesfaye thought, though he was made to appear a little Asian like the artist himself. He considered this now especially, as he reheated Chinese food in the microwave on the small cart under the portrait. The leftovers Tesfaye had brought back from his father's house were gone now and, living alone, he seldom cooked.

He grabbed his lunch plate and sat on the living room couch. Flipping the channels with the TV remote, he settled on CNN. He caught a story of actress Bethany Baird at a film festival with her newly adopted African daughter. The movie had been shot in the Horn of Africa and co-starred Ethiopian supermodel Liya Kebede.

Then came some more news about the fighting in Somalia, showing footage that included children alongside tanks in the road. Tesfaye recalled playing on wrecked tanks just like that.

After lunch and a shower, Tesfaye put on his new deep blue scrubs and left for work. While walking downstairs to his car, parked in the lot behind the building, he wondered whom he'd be working with tonight.

Hours later, he settled into his work routine in the ER. Thankfully, so far the summer night had been all right. Tesfaye sipped some of the coffee he had brewed and talked to Stephanie, his partner for second shift in the ER x-ray room.

"Did you do anything over the holiday weekend?" he asked.

"Nothing special, mostly I worked here. You know how much fun that is." Stephanie Walkowski hid her sweet, soft interior with a hard and sharp exterior, almost like a spiny lobster or some other sea creature. Her naturally jet black hair contrasted her porcelain doll complexion. She was big and curvy, with an uneven personality that vacillated from brassy and bold to shy and demure in a heartbeat. That quality made her a little hard for Tesfaye to deal with. Almost absentmindedly, Tesfaye clicked on the mouse of the image monitor, searching for examples of artifacts for his upcoming presentation. He stopped at a scapula x-ray, not really aware that Stephanie had done it earlier.

"Check this out," he said to Stephanie who was at the other computer. "Can you see how this fabric covers a scapular fracture on this x-ray," noted Tesfaye.

"Oh that's just a couple of pillows I was using to turn the guy up for the lateral view," she replied.

"But did you notice the fracture here? I wonder if the radiologist caught it. It goes through the acromion process. That's not something you see every day."

"No, I didn't see anything. I'm not surprised it's fractured though. That guy was hit pretty hard by an SUV's mirror. He was riding his bike by the stadium when it happened. Why do you care anyway? Let the docs do their job and we'll do ours," said Stephanie.

"It's just that I've agreed to talk about artifacts at the next meeting. I'm looking for examples to show."

"Well, you're not gonna use my x-rays, are you Tesfaye?!"

Not wanting to push it further, Tesfaye answered lightly, "I would never use your excellent work, Steph."

"Not very funny," she said.

Tesfaye chided himself for his naivety. He now saw that using examples of other technologists' work at this presentation would be a bumpy road. Some techs were bound to take it too personally. He realized with dismay that his presentation wasn't going to be as easy as he thought. Since he wanted a good working relationship with Stephanie, he let the subject drop. He promised himself that he would be more discreet.

Tesfaye was home by eleven-thirty that night. Tired from a full day of school and work, he collapsed on his couch with a beer and some pita bread. He turned on CNN Headline News. It took only a few swigs of beer and the hum of his air conditioner to put him in a relaxed state. He put down his drink on the coffee table. He stretched out on the couch, put his head back and dozed off into a dream.

Swirling colors blown by the wind. The sound of children's laughter. Running, running down a hard dirt road. Reaching, reaching for a scrap of paper flying in the breeze. Seeing black paper, carbon paper floating away. Chasing it, then falling, falling deeper into watery darkness. Engulfed by black liquid going down, going down. Can't breathe! Panic-stricken, struggle for life, must have air! Bottom felt at last. Feet push hard, push up hard, upward still. Light, then more light. Surface finally broken. Suck in air. Putrid air, smell of feces. Screaming women, yelling children. Help is coming, coming, coming, coming…

Tesfaye woke suddenly and stared at the TV, still tuned to CNN. The dream was a recurrent nightmare he hadn't had in years, one of those vestiges of childhood that linger deep inside the mind. But it stemmed from a real event, almost drowning in a trash pit outside a hospital back in Africa.

Gradually the dream faded from his mind. Deciding not to sleep anymore, he put a kettle of water on the stove to make tea. Then he remembered the dream again. He thought about the near drowning incident of his childhood. He recalled what he was trying to retrieve that day. It was carbon paper. Carbon paper that he used to make copies of his drawings and make-believe maps when he was a child. Tesfaye shook his head when he thought of the things that used to make him happy.

Chapter 15

Like two dogs about to be walked, panting and pacing, Muldoon and Koharski awaited the arrival of actress Bethany Baird. It was already two a.m.; Baird and Calabrey were thirty minutes late. The techs were holding a scan room opens for them. They were to enter through the propped open emergency exit door. In a moment Calabrey and Baird snuck in. Calabrey again in the lab coat, Baird covered by a blue surgery gown and cap.

With the click of the door they entered CT control. She ignored the hushed introductions, mesmerized instead by the sleek high tech room set in a relic of a building. With doors secured, Koharski announced they were ready. Baird peeled off the dull cap and gown and to the techs' jaw-dropped delight revealed a *People* magazine form resplendent with shoulder length chestnut hair, sprayed on tan and perfectly rounded, exposed attributes.

The warrior princess outfit, complete with daggers, beads and studded belt—a big hit with the drooling Muldoon—was completed with piercing rings in her ear cartilage and nostril. She looked like the character in her last film, *Return to Abyssinia*.

Muldoon capitalized on the actress's distraction with her surroundings by covertly popping out his cell phone. Standing tightly alongside her, he snapped an arm's length photo of himself with her. Baird recoiled, swore and turned to Calabrey.

"No pictures! Rod please, I told you no pictures. Rod, I don't like being here. It's the middle of the night and this place freaks me out." Calabrey reassured her, gently rubbing her shoulders.

Koharski escorted them into the scanner room. Calabrey described his vision to Baird. "I want to pose you with your arms crossed and the daggers in your hands. A defiant and fierce expression should be on your face. I want to arrange things just right."

"Wait. You mean I'm going to have to go into that big doughnut thing," protested Baird.

"Oh, yeah, but the scan only takes a few seconds really," answered Koharski.

"Rod, I can't do this," Baird pleaded. "I have claustrophobia," the actress pouted.

"Well, come now Bethany, are you sure? I mean, at least we could try. We could stop it when you wanted," Calabrey urged.

Under a silver wall crucifix that appeared as if had been there since the building was built a hundred years ago, Baird stood with arms folded, stage-prop daggers in both hands, biting her lip.

Koharski intervened. "Sometimes people are premedicated. That is, they take something to help them relax before we do a scan. Claustrophobia is not that uncommon, but like I said, the scan only takes a few seconds anyway."

"I do have some Ambicet here you could take," said Calabrey. He reached into his pocket, pulled out a small metal case. "I never know when I might need it." She rolled her eyes, reached up and took the pill from him. Koharski got a cup of water.

While they waited for the medication to kick in, the phone rang. As usual, the emergency room wanted to send over a case. Apparently a woman had arrived by ambulance after an MVA. They wanted a CT, head and neck, STAT.

"Can't do it right now, I have an ICU patient in the scanner. I'll call you as soon as we can," Koharski replied. Then turning to the others, "It's now or never, guys."

With the clanking of metal bracelets and the jingle of necklaces Baird wordlessly mounted the scanner table. Calabrey arranged her jewelry and clothing, positioning her like an Egyptian queen. Although Calabrey fussed over getting the pose just right, the scans were still completed in short order. Muldoon burned them onto a CD and Calabrey handed Koharski an envelope. He tore it open immediately.

"What's this? Another personal check? I thought I told you cash only!"

"You apparently had no difficulty cashing the last one, if I recall correctly," replied Calabrey.

Muldoon, who had returned to the scanner room to remove to the actress, interrupted them. "Houston we have a problem, better get over here right away!"

The three men gathered around the actress's now limp body. She was sound asleep. Koharski shook her. "Bethany wake up, wake up, we're done." Calabrey repeatedly brushed the strings of hair from his face.

"One Ambicet shouldn't have done this, unless of course, she had taken something before she got here," Koharski guessed.

"Well, perhaps she had a few drinks tonight," mumbled Calabrey. Muldoon stared at her body, then carried her to a stretcher, carefully putting her down like an overgrown child putting a doll to bed. He imagined what he could do with her now if only Calabrey was gone.

"Throw a sheet over her and take her around to the other scanner room and turn out the lights," Koharski commanded. Then going back into the control area, Koharski pointed at the opposite scan room and told Calabrey to stand behind the scanner. The phone rang just as he was reaching it to call the ER. It was the nursing supervisor. She wanted to know what the delay was. Koharski repeated the lie about the ICU patient but, sensing it wasn't enough, claimed the electricity had gone out momentarily. He added convincingly that, after the power was restored, they had difficulty rebooting the computers. Koharski ran his hand across the back of his shaved head. He told the supervisor to send the patient now.

As Rod Calabrey waited in the darkened room behind the older scanner, he clutched the CD and hoped that Bethany would forgive him. Once she sees the finished portrait all will be forgotten, he hoped.

A small contingent of nurses, attendants and an emergency room physician brought the car accident victim into the opposite scan room. Calabrey still hid in the darkened scan room. Baird lay on a cart next to him in a deep sleep. Across the way, Kathy Martin stood by to intubate the patient if necessary. The victim was a young woman, semi-conscious and still wearing the rigid cervical collar placed on her by the ambulance crew. The long bearded ER doctor, Mohamed Mughari, strode into the control room.

"We're very concerned about this woman. The EMTs said it was a terrible crash, a rear impact." Koharski nodded and began to set up the scan as Muldoon saved his cell phone photo. Calabrey worried in the darkened scan room that any moment he would be discovered. In rapid succession, the brain and cervical spine scans were completed and the ER team brought the patient out.

The physician turned to Muldoon. "Call me with that report from the Night Hawk radiologist as soon as possible." During the night, hospitals often utilized the services of radiologists, referred to as Night Hawks, as far away as Australia.

"Right, okay," Muldoon replied, now busy sending the cell photo to a friend. Next, they completed a scan of a second emergency room patient brought over immediately after the first. Patricia Coughlin was a sixty-two-year-old woman with a severe headache. It even hurt her to move her head.

Patricia Coughlin was spending the evening at her four-year-old granddaughter's birthday party when the pain began. She felt sorry about leaving the party early, but wanted to get back home and rest. Her home, a deep forest green, three story Victorian, was her best refuge from the chaotic, changing world outside. It was the only place she wanted to be when she felt ill. Mrs. Coughlin loved to sit in the breezy round turret room and listen to the B.B.C. on the radio as she knit things for the grandchildren.

She and her late husband had raised five boys in that house on the finest parkway in South Buffalo. One son became an attorney, one a councilman, another a policeman and still another a fireman. The greatest of loss of her life came when her fifth and last son died last year in a one-car crash. Even after that tragedy, Patricia Coughlin continued working at St. James the Great Parish, organizing donation drives for the poor.

Muldoon mocked her. "So you came in with a headache, did you think about taking an aspirin or two before you came into the emergency room?"

Patricia Coughlin closed her eyes and said the "Our Father" as Sean Muldoon moved her back onto her stretcher. He had Willie Stiles take her back to the ER.

After the emergency scans, the three men surrounded the stretcher where Bethany Baird lay. They shook her again. She opened her eyes weakly at first, and then wide open. She coughed, and then abruptly stopped coughing while her face flushed pink. Suddenly she began to choke.

"Do something!" Calabrey cried.

"Turn her on her side! She's aspirating her vomit!" shouted Koharski. The usually gorgeous actress gasped for air. Her face reddened. Then she coughed again, spitting up. Koharski wiped her face with a wet towel. Gradually Baird recovered. She sat up. Her color improved. She asked for a glass of water and where the bathroom was. Muldoon walked her to the toilet and slowly closed the door for her.

Koharski shook his head at Calabrey. "That's why they call them the weaker sex."

Later, after Calabrey and Baird were gone, Koharski let Muldoon have it.

"You and your fantastic ideas, Seannie-Boy! I should have learned by now to never listen to you. But no, I keep making the same mistake over and over!"

"What? Ron, everything worked out fine. It just took longer than we thought. And we got our money, buddy."

"Right you butthead. A personal check from an absolute stranger."

Chapter 16

"Hey, Muldoon, I heard you and Koharski had a bad MVA last night, a C-spine fracture?" asked Stephanie. Megan and Stephanie were ending their shift and about to clock out.

Muldoon replied, "Yeah, real bad. You know the fracture was hard to see on the cross table x-ray, so it was CT to the rescue again."

"Huh? You couldn't rescue a baby from its dirty diaper, Muldoon," replied Stephanie. Muldoon was known for his strong aversion to bad smells.

"You just wait till you need my help STEPH-A-KNEE!" With that, Muldoon left the breakroom to head over to CAT scan. Then Muldoon popped his head back in. "I almost forgot to show you my latest conquest." He pointed his cell phone at Stephanie and Megan, showing them a poorly lit photo.

"Who is that with you?" Megan asked.

"Who does she look like? It's Bethany Baird," bragged Muldoon.

"Let me see that. That's fake. You cut and pasted her face on your picture, then e-mailed it to yourself or something," Megan stated.

"Cut and paste, that sounds more like you, Megan. Cut and paste this!" cracked Muldoon.

"Believe me Muldoon, I would cut it if I could. Oh, oh, by the way did you talk to Gilbert yet? She was trying to get a hold of you. She was asking questions about last night."

Muldoon knew that Gilbert had called him three times.

"I must have missed her calls, no great loss there."

Down the hall Muldoon stepped into a darkened x-ray room shut down for the night. He listened to his voice mail. First, Gilbert said to please call her back. Then the next message sounded more urgent. She had questions about last night, about the power failure. Her third message sounded like a true emergency. She wanted to meet with Koharski and him at nine o'clock in her office the next morning. Feeling a burning sensation flush through him, Muldoon slammed the door open and went to CT.

-o-

Like the one who picks the short straw to muck out a horse's stall, it was Tesfaye's turn to work with Muldoon in CT. Coming into the control room, Muldoon saw Tesfaye sitting at the scanner workstation, going through random scans in preparation for his quality assurance presentation. He sought examples of artifacts on the images, such as safety pins or any external item that should have been removed prior to the study.

"Well, if it isn't the quality ASS-surance officer himself," Muldoon cracked. Tesfaye turned to greet Muldoon but Muldoon looked past him. On the monitor was a CT Tesfaye had just brought up. It was the topogram of Bethany Baird. Muldoon's

96

neck and face flushed, unable to conceal his shock. He pushed Tesfaye aside, sat in the chair and promptly erased the images. It all had happened so fast.

"I had to repeat that scan. That necklace and all that jewelry were under her blanket. Anyway, live and learn – right buddy?"

"Whatever you say, Sean. I wasn't here. I don't know anything about it." But Tesfaye had gleaned one peculiar thing about the image and it peaked his curiosity. That cross she was wearing, she had an Ethiopian cross around her neck.

"You know my mom had a cross necklace like that at home. Was the patient Ethiopian or something?" Tesfaye inquired.

"Are you kidding me? You're the only Ethiopian on this side of the planet, buddy."

Closing his eyes for a moment Tesfaye recalled the image. It wasn't just the cross that caught his eye. He'd seen what he thought were knives, a nose ring and earrings. But the most unusual thing was the topogram length. It was longer than he'd ever seen. And why do a topogram from head to knee? That was never the protocol. There was one more thing. Tesfaye had found the images in a computer folder labeled "emergency scan," along with a long accession number. This was not a registered patient he surmised. All registered patients had a medical record number along with a name.

Tesfaye kept those questions to himself, not wanting to upset the belligerent Muldoon further. After all, they had to work together all night and he knew Muldoon too well. The last thing he wanted was a confrontation with someone almost twice his size about vague suspicions that this particular scan was done intentionally or without authorization. Tesfaye knew he needed more information, more facts, and some kind of explanation.

Muldoon ignored him the rest of the night, which was fine with Tesfaye since he preferred not to be on the receiving end of one of his tirades. Muldoon reminded him of a vicious pit bull pacing its cage. Tesfaye wondered, *"Why should I care? Why should*

I care what happens when I'm not here?" Then he went to retrieve an emergency room patient for the next scan.

As Tesfaye took the old man's stretcher down the hall, the answer to his questions came to him. He leaned forward as he pushed, stopping at the CT door where Muldoon stood. Tesfaye found himself literally looking up from the point of view of a helpless patient into the wild-eyed Muldoon.

"What do we have here, Tesfaye? I think I x-rayed him last week. I took a bunch of x-rays – all negative, of course," said Muldoon. Then to the old man, "Why are you here again? I know you fell last week, but has anything changed?"

"I still feel lousy, and my head hurts," the old man said and then forced his eyes closed.

"Well this CT will cure you," Muldoon said facetiously.

When the old man's eyes closed it was as if Tesfaye's eyes had opened. He saw things with crystal clarity now. It had to stop. Muldoon had to be stopped. Muldoon had to be fired. The cruelty on those unable to defend themselves had to end. Tesfaye knew he could do it, if only he had the patience to wait for the right event, the right time to get unequivocal proof that Muldoon was a real liability to the hospital and those that depended on it. But then Tesfaye asked himself, *why me?* And he had only one answer, one that he really wasn't comfortable with. He told himself it was because *I'm an outsider in so many ways. I'm just passing through.*

Chapter 17

"Respiratory arrest..." Tesfaye began his report. He didn't like alphabetical order in English. With the last name of Ababa, he almost always had to go first. Today was no exception. "Respiratory arrest, myo...myocardial infarc...tion and stroke. Sorry, I'm a little bit nervous," he said. Oral presentations were not Tesfaye's strong suit and he knew it.

"Each one of these acute illnesses requires fast treatment. Now more than ever, doctors, nurses, EMTs and medical technologists, you know like myself, understand that to be true." Tesfaye paused to check his notes, took a breath in and continued. "In fact, actually, timing is so critical that at All Saints Hospital where I work there is always a 'stroke team' for each shift. Each member, including a CAT scan technologist, carries a page... a pager. The goal for a patient with a stroke could be to begin clot-busting drugs within an hour of arrival in the ER. What does this have to do with Cartography you ask? Well, I hope to show you that maps can present data to demonstrate how ERs, I mean, how emergency rooms serve their geographic regions. So I chose the headline from last week's paper *Emergency Rooms Flooded with Explosion, Crash Victims.*"

Tesfaye was getting warmed up and gaining confidence. He queued up the first "slide" of his Power Point presentation. To everyone's surprise it wasn't a chart or a map, but rather a CT scan slice of the brain.

"The white area of this CT brain slice shows blood pooling in somebody's skull. This person would not be a candidate for clot-busting drugs. Luckily, this patient got taken to surgery quickly, before permanent damage was done." Next, he flipped to a computer-generated map of the region.

"First, let me say that emergency rooms are great at gathering information—they have to be. So, patient information could be collected—collected without needing patient names.

"On this first map, I used the geographic information systems program, you know the G.I.S. in the lab, to make the concen...concentric rings shown around each ER. Since this is just a simulation, I removed some of the ERs to simplify things. Each ring represents a radius in the inc...increments of five miles with an ER as the center."

Flipping to the next image, a multicolored map, Tesfaye explained slowly, "Now we overlay the ringed distance map with population density data available through the U. S. Census Bureau. It's represented here as five density levels colored blue— light blue being the lowest density up to darkest blue being the highest density level. As you can see, the most densely populated areas don't exactly match with the concentric rings."

A reconstructed image of a crimson human heart with the coronary arteries cut open popped up on the projection screen.

"I just wanted to see if you guys were still paying attention," Tesfaye said with a laugh, now enjoying the class's stunned reaction.

"But seriously, this digital image depicts the veins, I mean arteries that bring blood to the heart muscle itself. You don't want to waste any time when these start to get clogged up." Several students smiled at Tesfaye's dry humor.

"Now back to the maps." Tesfaye clicked the laptop to the next page. Gradually filling in the map at individual points were small blood-red hearts. Professor Hornsby became suddenly more attentive. There had been times recently when he didn't know whether he was having angina or just gas. Hornsby folded his arms across his chest and then stroked his graying beard.

"Each small heart represents a patient who visited a local ER in the last 6 months. Remember, this is just a simulation—I don't have patients' addresses—but this information could be obtained for an actual study." The red hearts, as they appeared, didn't match the most densely populated areas. In addition, many of the hearts also appeared to be farther out from the hospital.

Since the chaotic night that All Saints ER had the previous week, due to the power failures, gas explosion and bush crash, Tesfaye had learned several things. One was that two inner city hospitals that did have power did not receive any victims from the two accidents. It was speculated that the ambulance crews just took them all to All Saints because it was the closest. And on any given night, the volunteer rescue squads from the surrounding suburbs were known to favor All Saints because of its proximity to their homes. They could drop the patient and get back home sooner. And some patients insisted on All Saints because they didn't want to go to inner city hospitals. To Tesfaye, this was unacceptable. As a worker who bore the brunt of this inequity, he was beginning to feel it was patently unfair and ignored by a hospital administration looking only at the bottom line. His presentation was one way that he could look at the situation objectively and learn from it. One encouraging result for him was that he now saw that his job was fairly secure, due to working at the busiest ER in the region.

"Notice that there are now population centers away from the city's center. But the ERs are...are basically near each other geographically, in the region's old city center. So, I think a study like this could be done to show the differences in volume of patients per ER, and, to compare actual ER locations to the population they serve. One last point I'd like to make is that drive time must be considered too. I mean drive time to the hospital. That too could be studied." Tesfaye flipped to his final image.

"You can probably tell that this is an x-ray of person's neck. It was taken after an MVA, I mean, motor vehicle accident. A standard x-ray for a common event, but notice that the vertebrae in the neck don't all line up. That's called subluxation and don't let it happen to you!" A few students laughed nervously.

"Thank you, Tesfaye. All right. Good. Very thoughtful. Any questions for him, people? Not one? Okay, next up is Michael Bowman," Professor Hornsby moved on to the next student.

Chapter 18

The Office of Ellen Gilbert

While Tesfaye was giving his presentation at the university, Ron Koharski was waiting for Sean Muldoon in their boss's small windowless office. As an overwhelmed radiology manager, Ellen Gilbert couldn't clear her desk from its piles of files, manuals and messages. A desktop computer had a screen-saver of a stony stream, complete with realistic trickling sounds. It reminded her of a tree-lined brook than ran through her parents' backyard outside the little village of West Falls. When she wanted to take off the many hats she wore as a department head, she gazed at the moving water and listened to its hypnotic murmur.

Muldoon stumbled in late for the appointment, complaining that he had just gotten off at seven a.m. His reddish stubble matched his pink eyes. Gilbert stood up as Muldoon sat down. She handed Muldoon a form.

"The nursing supervisor in the emergency room has done on incident report on a delay in CAT scan the night before last. I want you two to explain to me the reason for the delay."

Koharski spoke first. "We already told them we had an ICU patient on the table. Then after that the power tripped off. And, when the power came back on, the computers didn't reboot properly. We got multiple errors, and then the system failed the self-test. It took us three tries to get everything running again."

Now seated with her elbows on her desk, Ellen Gilbert tapped the tips of her thumbs on her nose.

"Are you guys sure you weren't playing poker or anything? I mean now that the patient has died, the ER is breathing down my neck." Ellen Gilbert hated being the department police officer.

Koharski rubbed his scalp. "What patient died?" he asked. "I heard it was a bad crash but she was all right when we scanned her." He glared at Muldoon.

"I heard it was a small fracture. Not a dangerous one," said Muldoon.

"You're thinking of the wrong patient. This patient was not in a crash," Gilbert said. "No, this patient had severe headaches. Her CT showed a subarachnoid hemorrhage, a burst aneurysm. The neurosurgeon claims that if he could have gotten her to the OR sooner, he could have saved her life."

Now Koharski remembered her, a little gray haired lady, early sixties with bad headaches. She said it even hurt when she moved her head. He never saw the CT himself. Muldoon sent it to the Night Hawk radiologist. Both men shifted in their seats, but didn't avert their gaze at Gilbert.

Muldoon said, "If there is anything we can do for you, I mean if you have any more questions, um, we'll be glad to help, Ellen."

"All right, I've taken notes on what you've told me. Ron, I need to talk to Sean alone for a minute. You're free to go." Koharski shut the door behind him.

"Sean, you don't have a stellar reputation around here." Muldoon smirked. "And although I haven't gotten any formal complaints about you lately, I want to see that you continue to stay out of trouble. The rumor mill says you're still rough with patients."

Babbling brook sounds emanated from the computer's screen-saver once again. Koharski once referred to it as "Ellen's psychobabble brook."

Muldoon raised his eyes to the ceiling, throwing his hands behind his head. Only one person came to his mind, Tesfaye Ababa. *He saw the scan. He blew me in. It must be him. What a freak. I'm gonna' kill him!*

"I don't care what people say, I'm good with patients, ask Ron." Muldoon was unaware that he had leaned forward with clenched fists, but Gilbert noticed his confrontational body language and sought immediately to bring the encounter to a close.

"Ellen, there's something I've been meaning to talk to you about," Muldoon said quietly.

"Go ahead."

"Well, you know how I don't like to talk about my coworkers. I mean we're all a team. We're in this together. But it's really been bothering me how Tesfaye doesn't do his share when we work together. He's not a team player. He makes a lot of tracking errors. And, he's too slow. It drives me crazy. He's just not cut out for hospital work. You should consider getting rid of him. And just between you and me, the patients still don't understand a word he says with that accent.

"Thank you for telling me. You guys are my eyes and ears. Without you, I really don't know what goes on. But let me get back to you, Sean. If these rumors about being rough with patients ever get substantiated, there will be an investigation. Please don't let me regret hiring you more than I already do."

That evening in between x-ray cases in the ER, Tesfaye roamed through previous exams to find artifacts on x-rays for his presentation. The monthly staff meeting wasn't for two weeks, but he wanted to be ready in advance. He didn't want his classes to suffer because of this.

Tesfaye printed up some examples including unexpected things on x-rays, like a disposable heat pack worn on the back of one patient. He decided to speak a little bit about new trends in artifacts such as dangling belly rings.

All the while he was skimming through the images on the computer, Megan McDonnell chattered. This girl loved to gossip, he thought. Tough on the outside, having grown up on the streets around the hospital, she seemed to Tesfaye to be a little bitter about her life. He wasn't quite sure why. Still, he enjoyed her company and they'd been through some brutal nights together in the ER.

Megan left to get a patient to x-ray his shoulder. At the nurses' station she ran into her sister, Kathy Martin, the respiratory therapist. Kathy greeted Tesfaye as he drove the portable machine by. The two women talked about Tesfaye. Kathy asked how long he had been working there and where he was from. When he returned from the portable exam, Megan flipped through an old *National Geographic*. Not her usual magazine of choice, she preferred *Us* or *People*. Tesfaye completed his computer tracking while Megan jumped back to the gossip, this time about Muldoon.

"Did you hear his girlfriend dumped him? You know her, my friend Melissa Adams over in medical records." Nodding, Tesfaye looked through his quality assurance manual.

"Yeah. How's she doing now? I heard she had gastritis or something."

"She's okay. But you know she'd be a lot better if Muldoon would just stop harassing her."

106

"It's always risky to date someone from work."

"You mean it's always risky to date Sean Muldoon." Megan held up the *National Geographic* for Tesfaye to see.

"Did you have lions near your village in Africa?"

This made Tesfaye laugh. What Americans think about Africans was always funny to him. "No, I only saw lions on TV until I went to a zoo at age thirteen. Actually, it wasn't a zoo; the lions were in a private collection that once belonged to Haile Selassie."

"High Lee who?" asked Megan.

"Haile Selassie, the last emperor of Ethiopia.

"The last emperor, that sounds like Japan not Africa."

"Well, Ethiopia had emperors too."

"Hey, were you one of those starving babies with the big bellies?"

Now getting a little bit perturbed, Tesfaye explained that sure, there were lions, droughts, famine, malaria and AIDS in Africa. But not everyone there experienced those things. He wondered if she thought that he used to run around naked in the brush. Megan apparently grew tired of the anthropology lesson and changed the subject.

"Did you hear that Muldoon is showing people a picture of himself with Bethany Baird on his cell phone? As if."

Although sometimes Tesfaye struggled with the stuff of small talk in American culture, he did know who Bethany Baird was. He'd even seen some of her pumped up action adventure movies.

Holding the phone now with Megan prattling on about Muldoon, Tesfaye dialed Ivan Denovich who was working over in CT. Denovich was the local CT expert.

"Yo Ivan, what's going on. Are we still playing chess next week? Same time? All right, man." Tesfaye admired Ivan for his knowledge of medical technology and his cunning at chess.

After Megan left the room, Tesfaye picked up the magazine and half-heartedly looked at photographs. He stopped at a page near the center. Something about it, he thought. Brown skinned African children surrounding a young attractive white woman on a dirt road in Somalia. She reminded him of Bethany Baird walking down village roads surrounded by the poor children of Ethiopian farmers. The rich attractive American white woman, a pied piper of sorts bestowing her time and money on the orphans of the Third World, coming to adopt one for herself, to rescue the child from the abyss of AIDS and starvation. Moreover, Bethany Baird had just returned from Ethiopia. He saw it on the news. *And Bethany Baird was with Muldoon?*

The connection didn't hit Tesfaye until he was driving home that night. A billboard with a model wearing a large gold cross triggered it. The scan that Muldoon rushed to erase, the topogram of a woman wearing an Ethiopian cross, a pendant with the arms of the cross bent upward to hold a large central disk. This cross design had been a symbol of Christianity in Ethiopia since the fourth century. Someone like Bethany Baird could buy one in Africa and wear it in the U. S.

Tesfaye thought, *that cell phone photo was real. She and Muldoon were together the night the topogram was done. Muldoon must have scanned her.* Tesfaye felt sure of it. *Why would she come to Buffalo though? Why would Muldoon scan her in secrecy? Maybe she had a medical condition that she was keeping out of the tabloids. How would Muldoon have met her? Perhaps through hospital administration or through Gilbert?* He made mental notes to ask Ivan about the long topogram without revealing his suspicions.

Chapter 19

Megan woke to the sound of breaking glass. With a chill running down her spine, she silently lifted her head from the pillow, straining to hear more. The neighborhood wasn't the innocent place of her childhood memories—if it ever was. Now break-ins on her street had become weekly occurrences and known drug dealers boldly stood on porches waiting for drive up drug sales. Her father no longer held for her a position of guardian or protector; if anything, she protected him.

For moments that seemed infinite, Meg heard nothing but the usual drone of the fan in her bedroom window. Gathering her courage, she quietly stepped from her bed, grabbed her robe and then went down the dark stairs to the first floor. Another crash, this time definitely coming from the kitchen, probably the sink. Meg wondered if her dad was up and around at this early morning hour. Not likely, she thought. Generally, he limited his movements to his chair in front of the TV, the bathroom and his bedroom. For several days now, he seemed more forgetful and confused. Meg accepted this as the natural course of an aging man with first stage Alzheimer's. His doctor told her it was too soon to tell if it was indeed Alzheimer's or perhaps an anxiety-depression disorder.

Clearly making out her father's distinctive "son of a pup," Meg became relieved and concerned all at the same time. As she rounded the corner into the light of the kitchen, Meg called out, "Dad, what are you doing up at this hour?"

"Huh, Oh Meggy, I was just a little hungry. Thought I'd make a sandwich."

Meg stopped dead in her tracks to avoid stepping on the broken glass in her bare feet. But something else stopped her too. Her father, in his feeble attempt to make a sandwich and get a drink, had made a huge mess in the kitchen. It was as if he had removed everything from the fridge and put it on the table.

"Dad, what are you doing? What a mess!" she yelled. Clearly, Meg thought, her father didn't know what he was doing. Now she felt guilty for yelling at him. Looking around, she saw no evidence that a sandwich was ever made, and he continued to take things from the fridge. In the past, her mother had done almost all the cooking, and then Meg took it upon herself to see that her dad got his meals.

"Meggy, can you help me find the mustard?"

"Dad," Meg said while slipping on her sandals. "We're all out of mustard. I'll get some this weekend, I promise. Sit down here now. I'll make you something, but first I need to sweep up the glass."

"Let your mother do that! Mary! Mary! Where is that woman?" he said, now sitting down.

"Dad, mom passed away four years ago. Don't you remember?"

"Huh? Oh, yes of course," her father said, now holding his head in his hands sadly at the cluttered table. Her mother and father had been a great match, Meg thought. Friends since childhood, and then reunited at a chance meeting at All Saints Cafeteria, they seemed destined for each other. There were tough times to be sure – for years they didn't own a car. Still throughout their marriage and her dad's unemployment, they loved each other in a forever kind of way.

Now, as heartbreaking as it was to remind her dad that his wife of thirty-two years was gone, it was even more painful for Meg to see him like this. Her father repetitively rubbed his hands together like they were cold. He had been confused and forgetful at times but this was a new level of incompetence that she could not ignore.

Megan put the broken glass in a paper bag and then into the garbage. Although she felt a wave of exhaustion and a sick feeling in the pit of her stomach, she was still determined to get this situation resolved for the time being and get back to bed. Meg had watched a movie until the wee hours of the morning, her usual habit after working until eleven at night. Normally, she would be sleeping in at this hour when many are rising to prepare for their workdays. Her dad ate some of the sandwich she made and then shuffled back to his bedroom.

What do I have to do? Put a lock on the refrigerator? Not one to give into self-pity, Meg decided to call her sister Kathy in a few hours after getting some more sleep. Kathy and Meg had bonded finally in the last few years after their mom died. They relied on each other now more than ever, sharing the burden that their father's illness produced.

Meg curled up in bed and reviewed her upcoming day. Rollerblading in the park would be nice, but now she was afraid to leave her dad alone too long. Then, there were the errands she needed to run before getting to work at three. She rolled onto the side she usually slept on but it was soon obvious there would be no more sleeping. Meg reached to her nightstand, and picked up her cell phone and called Kathy.

"Kathy, it's Megan. Sorry to call you so early." Kathy was currently in the throes of potty training her two year old. From the youthful protests in the background, it didn't sound like it was going too well. "Could you come over and check on Dad after I go to work? You know, make him some dinner, stay a short while, then settle him in his bed or set him in front of the TV? I'll be home after work at eleven fifteen."

"Hold on a second Meg. Heather! Heather, sit down there again. Stay there. Mommy will help you in a minute. Sorry, Meg, Heather wandered across the bathroom at a critical moment."

"It's okay. I think I got the picture," Megan admitted.

"Now, as far as tonight, I should be able to come around seven after everyone here has eaten. But tell me, what's going on?"

"I'm afraid to leave him alone for too long. A little while ago, he tried to make a sandwich and managed to empty the fridge onto the table and broke a plate and a glass in the process. Then he forgot that Mom was gone," complained Megan as she twirled her hair around her finger.

"I see — Heather! Be a big girl like Mommy and sit for just a minute — Meg, I'll be over at seven. We can talk about it then," said Kathy with a distracted voice.

"I'll be at work then, Kathy. I'll call you from there to go over this. We need to do something about Dad," said Megan before saying goodbye and closing her phone.

6:15 p.m. ER X-ray Room

The unkempt homeless, the smelly drunk, the unidentified car accident victim and even the abandoned infant each could be a "John Doe" or "Jane Doe" who ends up at the doors of All Saints Emergency Department. No one is happy to see them and for anyone new to hospital work, the weight of the words is even heavier.

"John Doe." The two words, there in black and white on the x-ray requisition, stood out starkly from the rest. "John Doe" with its implication of tragedy, loss, misfortune and mystery was a frightening term to the young Megan McDonnell. In her two and a half years of x-ray training, Meg never had to perform a procedure on one. It was not that she was squeamish, if anything she was not easily "grossed out." It was more that Megan felt deeply for the underdogs and the forgotten ones. To add to that, her inexperience led her to begin each shift with a pang of worry, a dread of what could possibly happen today. It seemed that so often, something bad did.

"Tesfaye, we gotta x-ray a 'John Doe.' Let's see, the requisition says found on sidewalk," said Megan. "Everything else is blank. No age, no address, nothin' at all. Can you help me with this?"

"Yeah, but what x-rays did they order?" asked Tesfaye.

"Oh, daaaahhh! Chest and c-spine, cross table. Both portables," said Megan with a slight tremor in her voice.

"Okay, just let me finish tracking my last case and then I'll be ready to go," said Tesfaye without looking up at Megan from the computer.

Megan drove the portable unit while Tesfaye checked the patient board in the nurses' station. A commotion outside one of the ER rooms led Megan to guess that the "John Doe" was in there being worked on. As she turned into the room before Tesfaye got there, she was momentarily confounded. Because of her inexperience, Meg had assumed all "John Does" were dead. A doctor, two nurses, two EMTs and an aide surrounded the stretcher, each attending to a task. Dr. Mughari lifted the man's eyelids to check his pupils. He simultaneously asked for vital signs. The intravenous line, put in by the EMT on the scene, was attached to a bag of fluid.

As Mughari spoke the words, "Okay, strong pulse but still unresponsive," he moved to the middle of the cart. Now having a clear view of "John Doe's" face, Meg froze. It can't be him, she thought. But then Megan McDonnell acknowledged the awful truth—it really was her dad.

Fleeing from the room she bumped into Tesfaye.

"You're...you're gonna have to...ummm...I mean, it's my, my Dad! I can't do it," cried Megan as she ran through the doorway.

Tesfaye's feeling of being torn between chasing after Megan or completing the x-rays were halted when Dr. Mughari told him to get over there and do the c-spine and stop wasting time. Mughari said that "John Doe" would go straight to CT after the neck x-ray was cleared.

"He's not a 'John Doe' anymore, doctor. I know who he is—he's Megan's McDonnell's father," said Tesfaye calmly.

Maintaining his composure, Tesfaye set up Mr. McDonnell's cervical spine x-ray and shot it with the portable unit. Mughari advised him that the chest x-ray could wait since his oxygen saturation and pulse were good.

When back in the x-ray room, Tesfaye saw Megan sobbing while on the phone with her sister.

"Kathy, Dad is here. Here in the ER," said Megan.

"What do you mean? Why is he—"

"—Kathy, he was found on the sidewalk a little while ago. It's all my fault; I should never have left him alone. He's unconscious now. Tesfaye just did his cross table c-spine x-ray," said Megan, making eye contact with Tesfaye.

After Megan got off the phone, she abruptly left the room saying only that she was going to see her father. Tesfaye reviewed the x-ray of her father's neck on the image monitor. All seven cervical vertebrae were visualized and aligned well, he thought. Most likely, her father's neck was fine. Tesfaye felt less than adequate at talking to Megan about her father and her life. Due to her tough nature, his current strategy was to just try to be a good listener. Tesfaye completed the computer tracking. Soon the radiologist would be analyzing the neck x-ray. Then, Tesfaye hoped, Mr. McDonnell would be on his way to CT.

The weekend that followed for Tesfaye revolved around uneventful work shifts alternated with late nights on the computer and sleeping in. Tesfaye heard that Megan's father had improved and was now conscious, though often confused about his whereabouts. His doctors were awaiting the opinion of a neurologist as to the exact nature of his condition. The differential diagnosis was simply an episode of syncope. Through the weekend, Tesfaye didn't cross paths with Sean Muldoon nor did he see Megan who had taken a few days off to be with her father. With the distractions of work and university assignments, Tesfaye gave no thought to Muldoon or his apparent scan of Bethany Baird.

Chapter 20

Sitting forward, Tesfaye stroked his thin goatee. Ivan had taken most of his chess pieces and it was now the endgame. Breaking from his contemplation, Tesfaye looked toward Ivan.

"Ivan, do you know why someone would do a long CT? I mean a topogram from the top of the head to the knees?"

Ivan stayed focused on the board. "This is a game you cannot win here. Sometimes better to resign and play a new game."

Ivan was right. All Tesfaye's pawns were blocked and Ivan had a passed pawn destined to become a queen.

"I don't know why anyone would do this type of scan. Sounds like it could be a mistake," said Ivan.

Later when the glasses were empty and the chess set put away, Tesfaye headed to the door. "Another lesson next week, Ivan? Same time?"

"Okay. Same time. But no more lessons, Tesfaye. You're getting too good for that."

September 11th Gallagher Beach, Buffalo,NY

Orange-red jet trails crisscrossed the darkening blue dome of the sky. Grey clouds hung in a diagonal wedge pointing northward. The laser patch of the setting sun burned through enough to make dappled reflections onto Lake Erie. Two windsurfers in wet suits angled back toward the rocky shore.

Gallagher Beach was not so much a beach as a waterfront reclaimed from the area's industrial past. Dredged and backfilled with similar sized boulders, the one mile stretch gave a slight semblance to a natural area. At one end of the stretch, the relic of an old rusty ship was moored alongside a large empty grain elevator, its concrete falling off in chunks. At the other end of the beach were marshy wetlands, undoubtedly polluted. Farther down the stretch lie the highways and railroads approaching the city.

The prominent feature of Gallagher Beach was its long wooden boardwalk, complete with a narrow fishing pier that stretched out into the water. At this pier's end, Tesfaye sat alone with his new fishing rod hoping to catch some small-mouth bass or yellow perch. He had wanted to fish ever since coming to America and finally he found a favorite spot. As he viewed the inspiring rays of setting sunlight, Tesfaye reminded himself that in the U.S. he could do things that he only dreamed of in Africa. Hunting, for example, was impossible growing up in Ethiopia. What was left of the wildlife lived on preserves in the southern part of the country. Basically, hunting had become illegal. Tesfaye hoped to buy a rifle and hunt deer in the autumn in the thick woodlands south of Buffalo. It wasn't quite the same as his childhood dreams of stalking elephants and lions on the savannah, but it was close enough.

After a little difficulty getting his reel unjammed, he baited his line, cast out and waited. Enjoying the summer evening, he propped his rod up and took out his earbuds and iPod. With African-born singer Gigi entertaining him, he couldn't hear someone coming up from behind. But he felt the dock shake with heavy steps.

Realizing he was no longer alone, Tesfaye cautiously turned to see the hulking figure of Muldoon bounding towards him. Tesfaye felt the first cool breeze of the night on his face as he removed his earbuds. In Sean Muldoon's determined expression, Tesfaye sensed hostility. But when Muldoon approached, he greeted Tesfaye with a laughing grin. Muldoon congratulated himself on his ability to track down his co-worker in just a few hours. Guessing that Ivan would have some clues to Tesfaye's whereabouts, Muldoon lied, saying that he had some money he owed Tesfaye and wanted to pay him back. Ivan suggested Gallagher Beach Pier.

"Everybody told me you liked to come here, Ababa, but I thought I'd find you spear fishing or something," said Muldoon, smoking a cigarette.

"I left my spears back home. What's up, man?"

"You and I, Ababa, need to have a little talk." Tesfaye picked up the smell of alcohol. "A little discussion about minding your own business," continued Muldoon.

He had seen Muldoon's antics before, but showing up now with a threatening tone was especially bizarre, even for him. A seagull coasted overhead, letting out a short cry. Tesfaye noticed how dark it was now.

"I don't know what you talk about," Tesfaye said.

Muldoon tossed the cigarette into the water and said, "Okay, enough of your crap. I know you went to Gilbert with stories about me."

"Oh, but that's not–"

"–You stay out of my life. Stay out and keep your mouth shut or you will regret it, mark my words. I could crush you with my bare hands. And, you know what Ababa? No one would care. Nobody. And don't forget, I'm buddies with every single cop in South Buffalo, so keep your big mouth shut."

Several cars sped by on the adjacent highway. Muldoon looked away from Tesfaye toward the parking area, appearing to be waiting for someone. And in that moment, Tesfaye thought maybe it was time to move on, to move to another city or move back to Rochester. He sometimes felt he was just passing through anyway. *What was there to stay here for?*

He shouted at Muldoon, "Man, you're crazy. Why don't you chill out?"

"Are *you* going to back off, or not Ababa?" Muldoon demanded through gritted teeth.

"I don't know what you're talking about."

Without warning, Muldoon shoved Tesfaye and his folding chair off the pier's end. For two helpless seconds, he was airborne. Tesfaye hit side-first against the water; the percussion blasted his eardrums. The splash flew above him and a burst of bubbles rose up. Plunging into cool and cloudy green depths, Tesfaye felt painful pressure inside his ears. The sky's light above grew dim as the bubbles diminished. Thick blackness surrounded him as he submerged.

Can't swim! Muldoon, you idiot! He panicked with arms clawing through boundless water. A desperate feeling overwhelmed him as his eyesight dimmed. *Is this the end?* With black below, dull green above, he struggled to kick, in weighted jeans. *The way it ends for me? Where is mom now? Dad?* He continued drifting downward. *Won't see grandma again? Does anyone know I'm here?* Unexpectedly, Tesfaye struck the bottom, feet first. He felt a rock. *Push up, push up!* He rose up quickly. There was light above him. He broke the surface, sucked a breath, and grabbed his chair. Muldoon's car tires squealed as he sped away. Tesfaye kicked and breathed and kicked. *Almost there! I can do this!* Using the chair as a float, he made it to a dock post, then to another, swimming short distances and then resting, calming himself at each post. *I'm gonna be okay. Did anyone see it happen?* The windsurfers were gone; no one was around. With one last burst of kicks, he would be at the rocks.

Finally, he pulled himself onto a slimy half submerged boulder. He slipped, struck his knee on the rock and then crawled on hands and knees through mossy driftwood, sharp-edged boulders and floating trash. At last on dry land, he stood up, clothes soaked and hands bleeding from abrasions. With shaky, clumsy footsteps, he stepped over tree branches, reminiscent of bleached leg and arm bones. From his hair and neck, he pulled wads of reeking green seaweed, its algae odor irritating his nostrils. Tesfaye wiped his wet face with a forearm. His breathing and heart rate slowed.

While walking carefully out on the dock again to get his rod and tackle box, Tesfaye originally felt no anger. He was mostly amazed he hadn't drowned. He also regretted telling Muldoon that he couldn't swim a few weeks earlier.

But by the time Tesfaye got to the car his feelings darkened and his adrenalin pumped again. The idea of buying a rifle again seemed very appealing. However, this time it wouldn't be for hunting, at least not for hunting animals. A perverse desire to hunt down and shoot Muldoon blew through his imagination like the wind now blowing off the lake. A chill set into him and he yearned to be dry and back home in his warm apartment. Tesfaye thought about his life's journey. He realized how much things had improved for him since he came to America. And he grew uncomfortable with his lust to kill Muldoon. It wasn't right and he knew it. It didn't fit into the life he had or the life he wanted. And things were basically good now, now that he was working and earning a living.

Tesfaye opened his car door and sat down to take off his dripping sneakers. He raised his eyes to see the full moon that had risen opposite the shoreline. It reassured him that the moon, sun and stars were the same ones that rose and set back home in Africa. By the time he locked his car doors and started the engine, he was feeling a little better, despite the violence of Muldoon's attack.

The hot shower back at his apartment felt wonderful but Tesfaye was restless. He couldn't settle down. He tried reading a chapter in his Environmental Science book and then flipped around channels on the TV. It didn't help. He couldn't distract himself from his anger toward Muldoon. He couldn't put it out of his mind. He wondered what to do the next time he saw him. Tesfaye decided that he would confront Muldoon, if for no other reason than to let Muldoon know he wasn't going to forget about it. He would tell him that the first chance he'd get; he'd get back at him. If it led to a fight at work and being fired, so be it.

Tesfaye put his book into his backpack and set the alarm for class the next morning. A pang of hunger reminded him that he hadn't eaten dinner. In the small bright kitchen, he reheated some leftover pasta, throwing a chunk of margarine in the pan with it. Taking the bowl into the living room, he sat at his desk and turned on the computer. There was something about eating alone that was the loneliest part of living alone for him. Tesfaye thought he'd never get used to it.

As his laptop monitor flickered to life, he remembered the Google Earth program he had installed the last time he used the computer. He finished the buttery pasta spiced with salt and pepper.

Setting the program's "fly to" destination to Addis Ababa, the capital of Ethiopia, he watched the green and blue globe zoom out of Western New York. It rotated clockwise, taking him on a simulated flight over the North Atlantic, then across North Africa to zoom down to Addis Ababa. He panned with the mouse down to Lake Zway with its adjacent volcano, one of a chain along the Great Rift Valley.

Then Tesfaye got creative. He reset his starting point to London's Heathrow Airport and his "fly to" destination to Addis Ababa. He took himself on the last leg of a return flight home. By rotating the viewing angle to the southeast and then skewing it to a bird's eye view, he recreated the journey. Racing beneath him was the English Channel, the forests of France and the white peaks of the Swiss Alps. He went down the boot of Italy to its heel and then hovered over the aqua expanse of the Mediterranean. After skirting the dry north coast of Egypt, he paused for a moment to zoom in on the Pyramids at Giza. Now following the Nile up through Sudan to the Blue Nile, Tesfaye continued to its headwaters at Lake Tana within the Ethiopian Plateau, not far from his birthplace.

On his virtual voyage, Tesfaye saw the waters of the Red Sea stretch for almost twelve hundred miles along the Africa's northeast coast. No doubt, he imagined, this was the route taken by Makeda, the legendary Queen of Sheba of the Old Testament, as she ventured from Ethiopia to meet King Solomon in Jerusalem. On her return trip back to the city of Aksum, she would have been pregnant with Solomon's son, Menelik, the future first king of a dynasty that would span almost uninterrupted for about two thousand years.

While Tesfaye played over in his head the rest of story, he set his sights on the massive ruins of Aksum with its ancient royal tombs and monolithic obelisks. In the legend as Tesfaye learned it, this was where Menelik, after returning from seeking out his father Solomon, kept the Ark of the Covenant. Menelik and his soldiers had taken the sacred gold-lined chest from Jerusalem. When Menelik returned with the acceptance of Solomon as his father and the Ark containing the Tablets of Law, he was proclaimed a hero and crowned king. The pride that Tesfaye felt over the story's link with the past was something he would always cherish. He zoomed the map out and rotated the globe back toward North America.

After he entered his current address, the program gradually closed in on the flat black roof of the long rectangular apartment building in which he lived. The circular shapes of the spruce trees lined the blacktop lot where his car was now parked. But this daytime aerial view image wasn't in real-time, and Tesfaye's car wasn't there. And in reality, he thought, his car and even his apartment building will never withstand the test of time like the legends of Ethiopia. He shut down his computer, turned off the living room lights and went to bed.

Chapter 21

In the upstairs flat of Sean Muldoon's parents' home, lights blazed even though it was four in the morning. Muldoon, just back from a night of drinking and carousing with his buddy Koharski, at first tried not to wake his sleeping parents and little sister in the apartment below. However, he got progressively louder with the things he did.

Divorced after a short three-year marriage, Sean Muldoon landed back in his childhood home last year, separated from the three daughters he cherished more than anyone. Both sides hurled accusations of infidelity during the divorce proceedings. When the dust settled, Muldoon's mother accepted him back with open arms. His father, a retired fireman disabled on the job from a fall off a ladder, was less than enthusiastic about welcoming his prodigal son. He thought he was done with being woken up at night and done with all of Sean's elaborate excuses.

Upstairs, Sean Muldoon whistled as he emptied his pockets of change, keys and wallet. Then he grinned mischievously as he counted the cash that Koharski and he had garnered from selling acquired metropasses and DVDs. Although the profit paled in comparison to their new CT scan windfall, the sales made great beer and gadget money. Koharski had a friend at the county social services building who got him a monthly supply of the "extra" passes. However, Ron Koharski preferred to rely on his friend Muldoon for dispensing the pass cards.

Taking the TV remote from the littered coffee table, he flipped on wrestling and went into the kitchen. Grabbing a bag of hot and spicy chips from the cabinet, Muldoon chuckled in amusement when he recalled Tesfaye Ababa's sprawling plunge into Lake Erie. *That'll teach him to mess with this big boy*, thought Muldoon.

Munching away, Muldoon stripped down to his briefs. Within the sea of freckles on his right shoulder was his only tattoo. It was a leprechaun with fists ready, the symbol of the fighting Irish of Notre Dame. As a teenager, he worked towards his dream of attending Notre Dame. He got the grades he needed. He even got the interview. The rejection by the admissions department resulted from a simple phone call to one of Sean's references that revealed that he had assaulted teachers on two separate occasions. But by then, he already had the tattoo.

From a cheap wooden shelf unit next to the TV, Sean Muldoon picked up his favorite new toy. Shaped like a short baseball bat with small control buttons, this device along with its companion computer could be used to interact with a variety of virtual reality scenarios on the television. Pointing the cream-colored plastic wand at the screen, Muldoon selected the Black Hole Bloodbath game and then his opponent Kobalt, a two-head blue alien. He considered playing Terror Threat Three because it had just been September 11th, but he'd grown tired of fighting people with hooded faces. In an inspired moment a few weeks ago, he realized that to be the major flaw of the game—and told everyone his theory.

"You've got to see their facial expressions when you hit them or stab them. That's a big part of it. Without that, a game sucks," elaborated Muldoon to his friends.

Muldoon readied himself in his starting position. Standing sideways to the screen, he set his right arm and leg forward and his left arm and leg back. Before hitting the start game button, he adjusted his underpants with his left hand and then squatted down slightly.

"You will pay for the sins of Mankind," the alien heads warned in unison when he hit the start button. "Human, be prepared to die."

Loud buzzing emanated from the TV's stereo speakers. The alien swung his light saber across; only to be met by Muldoon's with a loud sparking sizzle. Now Muldoon countered with a jab, only to be stopped by the alien's quick reflexes. Muldoon focused on his wand for a moment to pause the game. Meanwhile, the alien delivered a scoring blow on Muldoon. Swearing, Muldoon paused the game and reset it to an easier level.

Once again assuming his sideways starting stance, he began play again. This time the alien was noticeably slower and Muldoon aimed to make him pay dearly for the previous attack. Kobalt's blue alien skin turned to crispy black burns each time Muldoon connected. Soon, green liquid trickled from Kobalt's wounds. The creature bared its two sets of teeth in dog-like growls and then let out a pained yelp each time it was struck.

Now really fired up, Muldoon guessed that only two or three torso hits should be enough to finish off the alien. Dodging a mid-section swipe, Muldoon then spun around into a forward lunge, stubbing his little toe on the couch leg. Stumbling onto the couch, he cursed and reached for his injured foot with his left hand, still holding the wand in his right. The now burned, blue alien's four eyes glowed orange as it began a diagonal swing to capitalize on Muldoon's immobility. Letting go of his foot in the nick of time, Muldoon pressed the wand's button to pause the game.

Downstairs, Sean Muldoon's middle-aged parents awoke to the commotion coming from the room above them. His father turned over in their bed and vented to his wife.

"When I see Sean in the morning, I'm gonna kick him outa here once and for all. I've had enough. What's he doing up there at this hour anyway?"

Sean's mother whispered, "He's probably just playing some game on his TV. You know how he loves those computer games. Just go back to sleep. Let me talk to him in the morning. You know how upset you get when you talk to him. It will only make things worse."

Chapter 22

Tesfaye stacked up x-ray cassettes to prepare for a multiple exam case. He calmly reflected on how life goes on for weeks or even months without a major occasion. Then, sometimes planned and sometimes not, events merge or converge to create the "big day," a pivotal day. And so often, that "big day" can involve someone from a radiology department. What may be "just another day," for x-ray technologists, can end up being a memorable one for their patients. It could be a bride's mother becoming ill at the reception, or it could be the bride herself, in her wedding gown, after she slipped and fell on the dance floor. It can be a child's first time skiing or a father's last time down the slopes. And sometimes it might be the day a grandmother got her new hip or a newborn fought for survival. For Tesfaye's current patient, it was just that kind of day. In fact, it was a very lucky day for him, one that he would never forget. Having fallen sixteen feet when his ladder slid off the end of the rain gutter, the man landed flat on his back on soft shrubbery. Other than having the wind knocked out of him and getting scratched up, he was uninjured.

Tesfaye's patient winced slightly as he wriggled himself off the stretcher toward the x-ray table. The requisition called for right ribs, lumbar spine and a chest x-ray. Tesfaye sought out an angle sponge and brought the x-ray tube over the patient and to begin the rib series.

A fall can be devastating, Tesfaye thought, thankful that he had landed in water the night before. Other than the cuts on his hands, he was okay. When he stopped at the police station, an imposing armory-like building along a block of boarded up storefronts, the officer appeared unimpressed by his story. The cop said that since there were no witnesses and no serious injuries that it would be best to forget about it.

But Tesfaye knew he would never forget. How could he, he thought. It only strengthened his resolve to go after Muldoon. But what did he have so far? A scan of an actress, rough treatment of patients, being pushed off a dock? He doubted anyone would care.

Tesfaye's deliberations were interrupted when Kevin returned from surgery. He had been to an OR case that required the x-ray C-arm equipment. Tesfaye finished the lateral lumbar radiograph and together he and Kevin moved the injured man back to the stretcher. When the workflow slowed down, Tesfaye had the chance to tell Kevin the whole story.

"Somebody's got to do something about Sean Muldoon. That guy's crazy," began Tesfaye as Kevin straightened up the x-ray room from the last case.

"I know he's crazy. What did he do now?"

"Just try to kill me. That's all," said Tesfaye with a smile.

"What? He tried to kill you?"

"That's right. I was fishing last night. You know, at the dock I like to go to, near those new windmills on the lake. He shows up and starts saying crazy things like I better stop complaining to Gilbert about him. Man, he's nuts. You know what he did? He blew up and kicked me and my chair off the edge."

"Whoa. Tesfaye. You're telling me he attacked you last night?"

"Right. That's exactly what I'm saying."

"Did you call the police? Did you report it?"

"I went to the police station and they pretty much blew me off. They said they'd look into it. But, to tell you the truth, I think they'll file the report in the garbage can."

"Wait. Did Muldoon know you can't swim?"

"That's something I don't know. I'm still thinking about that. But, you know what's kind of funny?" Tesfaye paused. Kevin listened; amazed that Tesfaye could find anything funny about it. "I think can swim now, I mean not too well, but enough so that I didn't drown last night."

"Ah. But the whole thing sounds awful. Did anybody see it happen? Have you told anybody else about it?"

"No man, nobody. And I'm not going to Gilbert. She's useless. Other than you, I might tell Meg about it, but she's got enough problems of her own, you know, with her dad. Anyway, she's taken time off to be with him. But there's something else I got to tell you about. Something is going on with Muldoon," said Tesfaye, lowering his voice.

"Go ahead."

"Remember how he showed people a photo of himself with Bethany Baird?"

"Sure, nobody believes it's real though," replied Kevin.

"Well it is. I mean he was with her."

"He ran into her somewhere?"

"No, I think she came here. I think she came to CT. And something else, I think he did a CT scan of her." Tesfaye explained about seeing the Ethiopian pendant cross on a female's topogram and its link to the actress.

"I don't get," started Kevin again. "Why would he have scanned her? And why wouldn't he have taken off her necklace beforehand?"

Tesfaye and Kevin had no answers, just more questions. They talked about what they could do about Muldoon, going over the attack again in more detail and his general bullying of others.

Kevin Connors took off his glasses and wondered aloud to Tesfaye, "Why is it that all these out of control, testosterone-overloaded hotshots always sound alike with their intimidating threats? What was it that he said to you before he knocked you into the water? Something like, I'll crush you with my bare hands?" And then Kevin continued emphatically, "And how many times, since I was a kid, have I had to listen to their know-it-all arguments or their apologetic excuses when finally outnumbered and backed into a corner."

As Kevin cooled off, Tesfaye explained that Muldoon had erased Baird's CT scan. Tesfaye also pointed out that it was in an emergency scan folder. Kevin guessed that it might be possible to retrieve the deleted scan. He believed it involved several computer steps but it could be done. Promising to help however he could, Kevin said he would try to get Ivan's help Friday when he worked with him. Neither one knew where the retrieval of the topograms would lead them.

Chapter 23

On Friday evening in CT, Kevin Connors found not one, but two files named emergency scans. But, as expected there appeared to be no images in the folders. Ivan sat back in his chair with arms folded as he walked Kevin through the steps necessary to restore rejected images. Almost everything Kevin had learned about CT, he had learned from Ivan. But it had been a long process because Kevin only worked part time for All Saints while teaching at Sinclair College. And it hadn't been easy. Kevin was more demanding as a student than most and Ivan was less extroverted than your typical teacher. Kevin always felt like he asked one too many questions. At times, their relationship felt strained to him. And sometimes Kevin wondered if Ivan simply resented his proctor role or if it was really something deeper, something private related to Ivan's previous life in Russia.

"Now, open the file marked 'd:PTEMGCY,'" said Ivan,

carefully pronouncing each letter to overcome his Russian accent.

"You should see those two emergency folders inside it. You have to go into each folder, and then each image separately. Type in 'completed' on the lines that now say 'rejected,'" continued Ivan.

Finally, with one last double click of the mouse to restart the image viewer, a topogram appeared on the monitor. But it wasn't what Kevin expected. It wasn't the actress, as Tesfaye described. It was a fully clothed male, complete with glasses, scanned from head to knee. The overview image was peculiar. It seemed almost like the man was posing with one hand on his chin and the other across his abdomen.

"What do make of that, Ivan?" Ivan didn't respond immediately; he was studying the image closely.

Kevin again commented on the image. "Do you see what I mean? Look—he's still got his clothes and glasses on!"

Ivan just said, "I don't know what this scan is for. But it's not for medical reasons."

Repeating the procedure for the second file, Kevin restored Bethany Baird's scan. Kevin had grown accustomed to the high-resolution topograms that the new scanner could produce, but now he was viewing something different. It was a celebrity's flesh and bones. Not that you could really tell it was Bethany Baird, but all CT scans were still magical to Kevin to some degree.

After printing the images, he deleted them once again, so as not to be discovered by Muldoon. Ivan sat quietly, studying newspaper ads. Kevin went to the file office to get the printed topograms. Then Kevin read the date of the actress' scan on the bottom of the printed film. It was the night of the incident, the night of the power failure, the night the patient with the burst aneurysm died before getting to the OR. It was the night that Muldoon and Koharski were later grilled about delays in CT.

Pushing the films into an envelope, Kevin walked back into CT. Tesfaye had gone to see his father for the night. Kevin planned to give Tesfaye the films Sunday when they next worked together.

10:10 p.m. The Studio of Rod Calabrey, New York

The rain pelted the oversized windows of the second story Manhattan brownstone. Guests who dared sampled sushi and sipped saki. Others stuck with cheddar cheese and pinot grigio.

Several partitions divided up the spacious loft, reclaimed from early 20th century office space. Each partition contained large paintings of human figures. A half circle of visitors gathered around Rod Calabrey as he discussed his latest creations. The two full-length portraits on frosted glass in multi-colored transparent inks stared back ghoulishly from their eye sockets. Each had its own backlighting to help reveal bone, flesh and clothing with shocking precision.

Calabrey, bathed in the stained glass glow of the portraits, was in his glory. Bethany Baird, with her new baby and new boyfriend in tow, heaped praise on him and his work. To top it off, a photojournalist from *Art News* was expected to do a special feature. Across the glossy hardwood came Derrick Perry, known as D'Rick, and his socialite mother, Sharon Peters. D'Rick, a white rap recording artist, had just returned from touring Japan and Australia. With his mouth full of hors d'oeuvres, D'Rick complimented Calabrey's portraits in his own inimitable way.

"There's one thing I know, that's what D'Rick likes and D'Rick likes that," he said pointing to the portrait of Baird. D'Rick usually spoke and sang with words not found in any dictionary describing a gang culture that he could only imagine.

"Your work is magical, Rod," said D'Rick's mother.

"Hello there, Sharon, and thank you. I'm so delighted you could make it here tonight," Calabrey greeted Sharon. After introductions, again the attention turned to Calabrey.

"Rod, I can totally see you getting into the Museum of Modern Art. Can't you see these pictures getting you in there?" Bethany remarked.

"I hope you're right, my love." For Calabrey, getting into "MOMA" would be like a lifetime achievement Oscar. For his entire adult life, Rod Calabrey dreamed of being hailed as a master, put alongside the likes of Pollack and Picasso.

D'Rick's mother, Sharon, appeared only slightly older than her son. Clad in a black silk dress, trimmed with a low neckline of black fur, her plastic surgeon was literally one of her best friends.

"The paintings are really awesome. There's almost a medical quality to them. And a high tech look to them as well." Turning to her celebrity son, she blurted out an idea as if it were an epiphany.

"Derrick, imagine a portrait of D'Rick done like this, with sunglasses, guns and splattered paints. It would be great as a billboard. Maybe your website." Her son's mouth was too full to respond. "No wait, your next tour – each concert could use a projected image of you like this. We'll mix it with video of you surrounded by police. Then more video with surgeons, nurses and medical equipment—maybe in an operating room."

D'Rick swallowed. "Like I survived. I fought and survived the fight of my life." He started to chant, "Blood on my chest. My near-death. Don't ya know it's my last breath. I see the dark. I see the light. Talkin' to God all through the night."

Then turning to the artist, "Can you do it, Mr. Calabrey? Can you do D'Rick?"

Chapter 24

Between the pale green surgical mask and cap, Tesfaye Ababa's burnt sienna eyes strained to estimate the correct centering for the next x-ray. The lanky orthopedic surgeon, Dr. Banes, was quickly losing patience with him and Tesfaye knew it.

"Lower the c-arm. Now go proximal! Toward the femoral head. Picture. Picture!" said Banes with his nasal voice.

Tesfaye was, practically speaking, between a rock and a hard spot, having trouble aligning the x-ray c-arm with the patient's hip joint. He stood between the elevated, slightly spread legs of a rigid elderly man whom Banes was operating on. Due to this rigidity, Banes was unable to give Tesfaye adequate space to manipulate the sweeping six-foot "C" shaped portable x-ray equipment. Every time Tesfaye rotated the curved arm back down to the lateral projection and directed it toward the patient's groin, he brushed the "C" along the unaffected leg.

Though it was not his fault, Tesfaye bore the hostile result of the limited workspace. And if Tesfaye had more experience, he may have insisted that the patient's legs be spread farther. It took him longer than usual to change the x-ray tube position and now Tesfaye heard anger in the surgeon's voice coming from behind the long clear plastic drape that separated them.

"Go to the AP now! I said, AP!" snarled Banes, asking for a frontal view. Banes had drilled the last of three long wires through the femoral neck into the head of the femur.

"All right. I heard you the first time," replied Tesfaye without malice, trying his best not to break the man's other leg as once again the c-arm pressed against it. Tesfaye had worked in surgery before, and had done hips with Dr. Banes, but had never seen him so aggravated before. Through the course of the operation, the conversation eventually revealed that Banes had struggled with the previous case, a femoral rod replacement, for hours and was spent. Palpable tension was felt in the room by the anesthesiologist, the circulating nurse and the OR tech as Banes waited for Tesfaye to bring the tube above the patient. The only sound was the whooshing of the suction tube. Finally, Banes could hold it in no longer.

"Listen. Is there somebody over in x-ray that knows how to operate this equipment? I mean this is totally unacceptable!" said Banes. He turned to the circulating nurse. "Call over to x-ray and have them send someone else!"

Tesfaye spoke up, saying firmly, "I'm it. There is no one else." He pressed the exposure button; the black and white monitor flashed a perfectly centered hip image.

"Good. Never mind about calling x-ray," said Banes, now softening and pleased with his wire positions. "I'm sorry," he peered over the plastic drape and said to Tesfaye, "What's your name?"

"Tesfaye Ababa."

"Okay, Tesfaye. I think you'll do fine. I appreciate your help. I'm sorry I couldn't give you any more space there, but you know, his fracture is so well reduced – I didn't want to displace it."

"No problem. You got the tough job."

Banes used a long hollow drill bit over the wires to prepare for the next step. Leaving the wires in for guidance, he screwed in three hollow or cannulated screws. Then he removed the wires. After two final pictures, Tesfaye's participation in the surgery was over.

Tesfaye let out a breath held in too long. Feeling tightness in his shoulders, he reached upwards and then outwards with his arms in a stress relieving stretch.

Tesfaye came back to the x-ray department and removed his lead apron, mask and cap. He wondered how things were going down in the ER with Megan and Sean Muldoon. He hadn't seen Muldoon since the night of the attack at the pier. His adrenalin pumped every time he thought about it. Still, Tesfaye didn't want to confront him now, the timing wasn't right. He planned on waiting to see if Kevin had retrieved the erased topograms before he could take a next step. One way or another, those images could be the key, he thought, to ending Sean Muldoon's pattern of abuse at All Saints Hospital. Tesfaye also hadn't seen Megan since her father's hospitalization and he really wanted to tell her about the attack, but hadn't had the chance.

Ron Koharski limped into the control room, returning from an ICU portable chest x-ray. Koharski seemed particularly edgy, like something was eating at him. He dropped two x-ray cassettes on the counter with a bang. After plucking two more requisitions off the printer, he swore.

Tesfaye asked, "Yo, Ron what's going on?"

"Ahhh. More freakin' STAT portables. How's Dr. Banes today?" asked Koharski, leaning over to rub his knee.

"Banes? Like Dr. Jekyll and Mr. Hyde. But, today he was okay. What's up with your knee?"

138

"It's killing me. Torn cartilage. I'm having arthroscopic surgery next month," explained Koharski, now slamming his cassettes onto the digitizer tray. Koharski sat down, sighed, and reached for his crossword puzzle.

"Next month? That's a long time to wait when you're in pain."

"You're telling me? Listen, the hydrocodone's not even touching it, not even close," complained Koharski and then began to concentrate on the puzzle.

Tesfaye tracked his hip surgery case on the computer and then asked, "Mind if I go take my break now?"

"Yeah, you go ahead. And when you're done, will go relieve McDonnell and Muldoon in the ER for dinner?"

"All right, man," said Tesfaye, wasting no time in starting for the cafeteria.

Over in the ER x-ray room, Megan McDonnell regretted wearing her new deep pink scrubs this particular evening. She caught her reflection in the mirror before leaving for work and thought she looked better than ever in them, with her light hair and slightly tanned skin. But in fact, once she started working, she thought she looked too good, because Sean Muldoon seemed to be buzzing around her like a bee by a cola can. He was behaving like a schoolboy with a crush. He tried to impress her in every possible way. First, it was his knowledge of anatomy, picked up in CT. Then, it was how much money he was making by picking up extra shifts. Lastly, he even pulled up his sleeve to flex his bicep. Megan laughed through all this, even though she found his personality repulsive. Muldoon stood closely at her shoulder as she reviewed her last patient's wrist x-rays at the monitor.

"Let's go out drinking after work. You and me. We'll start out across the street at Doc Murphy's. Then, maybe we'll head to a club downtown?" Muldoon asked with intent eyes on Megan.

Megan frowned at him. "I thought you didn't go to clubs downtown. That you liked to stay over here?" asked Megan skeptically.

"Usually. You know, I can walk into any bar around here and people know me. We have a great time. But downtown, that's a different story. It's like this; I'd rather be a big fish in a little pond than a little fish in a big pond."

"Reminds me of a song my mom used to sing. Something like 'I'd rather be a hammer than a nail,'" said Megan.

Sean Muldoon broke out in song: *"I'd rather be a hammer than a nail. Yes, I would. If I only cooouuuldd. I surely wooouuuldd."*

"Sounds like the story of your life. Your motto," Megan said. She knew the two sides of Sean Muldoon and wasn't budging. "I'm going to get the next patient," she said quickly.

In the presence of pain, the personality differences between Megan McDonnell and Sean Muldoon became clearer. Megan dodged a housekeeper with his cleaning cart, as she pushed her next patient, curled into a fetal position, through the doors and into the x-ray room.

"What took you so long?" asked Muldoon.

"What's that supposed to mean, Sean? Are you saying I'm too slow or something?" Megan challenged. Muldoon didn't reply.

Megan continued, "For your information, I waited for the nurse to give this gentleman his pain shot."

Muldoon's spoke through his teeth. "That's not the way we do things down here. We don't have time for that!"

"What are you talking about, we're not even that busy now."

Muldoon's face reddened and said in front of the distressed patient, still doubled over in pain, "Listen to me." He pointed a finger at Megan and then the patient before continuing. "This guy's probably just a drug seeker. He just came in for a fix. Once he gets something strong, he'll be running outa here! Mark my words."

"Drug seeker? You idiot! I've known Mr. Sullivan here my whole life. His daughter's one of my best friends. I know this man! He's got another kidney stone!" Now Megan's face was flushed as pink as her scrubs.

"Megan, who is this guy?" asked Sullivan weakly.

"Pay no attention to the man behind the glass," said Megan with a silly deep voice as she noticed Muldoon had slipped away. From behind the large window separating the x-ray table from the control panel, Sean Muldoon glared at her.

"You should be feeling better once the medicine kicks in. Do you think you can slide yourself over to the x-ray table?" she said.

"I'll try," groaned the patient. The door to the x-ray room slammed. Muldoon had walked out.

While Meg centered the x-ray tube over the abdomen of her now relaxed patient, she pushed Muldoon out of her mind. But then she wondered, why it is, that when some people encounter others with pain, they quickly dismiss it as either trivial or just an obstacle. Megan had seen firsthand her mother suffer through months of pain before she died. Her dad, Kathy and Meg each did everything they could to make her comfortable. Meg knew instinctively that her hardworking mom's pain was real. And Meg suffered emotionally too, when her mom's gall bladder surgery at All Saints found the cancer ravaging her insides.

Meg pressed the exposure button. The control panel buzzed for a one second as the radiation went through Mr. Sullivan to create the radiograph required. Meg questioned herself as to if she'll ever get hardened to others' pain after she puts in years as an x-ray tech. And then she wondered if there's any hope for the Sean Muldoons of the world. Can they become more empathetic or is it a lost cause? Her last thoughts went tangentially, as she pondered if there really was such a thing as a "high tolerance" for pain and how do you tell the degree of another's pain. After the x-ray cassette was digitized, Megan studied Mr. Sullivan's kidneys on the monitor. She magnified the image and adjusted the contrast on the bean-shaped glands. Within the right kidney, Meg discovered a staghorn calculus, a large pointed kidney stone, a rare occurrence but not all that unusual for Patrick Sullivan.

As Megan pushed Mr. Sullivan's stretcher again past Jack from housekeeping and then Dr. Mughari in his lab coat, she got big hellos from each one. Using the large circular wall mirror at the corridor's intersection to prevent a collision with a little boy in a wheelchair, she saw the pink reflection she created. She felt proud to be part of All Saints ER. After wishing Sullivan a speedy recovery and returning him to his bay, she noted a few EMTs lined up with patients in the ER hallway, ready for a preliminary evaluation. Bob the old security guard saluted her. She remembered that Bob and her mom were good friends long ago. Megan smelled the pizza that the nurses and clerks were nibbling on before she even stepped into the nurses' station. Seeing her sister Kathy chatting with the secretary, Megan snuck up behind her and pulled on her stethoscope.

"Hey sis!" said Kathy. "I didn't know you were on tonight. How's it going?"

"Okay, nothing I can't handle," replied Meg glumly.

Kathy pulled her black hair around her ear. "Doesn't look too bad," she said, motioning to the patient board. The dry-erase patient board with nurse assignments was only half full.

"Still, I'm a little nervous about tonight. It's my first night back since dad got sick and I'm a little stressed."

Kathy leaned away from the secretary. She whispered, "It's Sean Muldoon, isn't it?"

"Basically. Yeah. He makes my skin crawl. But I'm glad to see you Kathy. Thanks again for taking charge of dad's care." For a moment Meg leaned her head on her sister's shoulder.

"Don't say another word about it. And chin up!" teased Kathy.

Megan smiled, helped herself to a slice of pizza and walked back towards the x-ray room. She paused at a smaller dry-erase board near the waiting room. It read in fanciful blue handwriting, "Welcome to All Saints Hospital. Your doctor for today is Dr. Mughari. Charge Nurse is Mike Delaney. Respiratory Therapist is

Kathy Martin. Aides are Jose' and Janine." Taking the blue marker, Meg wrote with a squeak, "X-ray Tech is Megan McDonnell." And she drew a little bone next to her name.

Through the hall she walked again, feeling happier. For any new employee, work has its ups and downs. But for Megan McDonnell, All Saints Hospital represented more than work. As early as she could remember it was a heartwarming fixture in her life, like a miniature ceramic village put out at Christmastime.

Every Saturday as a kid, Megan, her sister and her dad would walk down their street to meet her mom for lunch in the cafeteria. And that was just one of many fond memories. Though Megan never actually realized it, she loved All Saints Hospital. She loved it for the Irish Dancers with their bouncing curls and clicking heels in the lobby every St. Patrick's Day. She loved it for the shiny tropical green display of large palm branches in the atrium every Palm Sunday. And she loved it for the crunchy ashes smeared on foreheads on Ash Wednesday. It wasn't all just memories either. It was traditions and it was real people. She cared about real people like the silver-haired volunteers in their red jackets in the gift shop. She knew real people like Bob the security guard and Jack the quirky cleaning guy. And she knew and cared about patients like Pat Sullivan with his awful recurring kidney stones. Megan never thought about these things consciously. They were deep in the realm of things that make up who a person is and far removed from who a person wants to be. But for every reason that Megan McDonnell loved All Saints Hospital, Sean Muldoon couldn't care any less.

Although both he and Megan grew up on the streets nearby, All Saints was a different kind of place for Sean Muldoon. For Muldoon, it was a place to make and use his connections. It was a place to exert control and a place through which he could conquer women and acquire possessions. And some part of Sean Muldoon believed that it was the place that he could make everything in his life right again, even if he hurt people in the process.

Tesfaye found Megan munching on pizza and flipping through *People* magazine in the ER x-ray room. Seeing Tesfaye, she looked up, her cool blue eyes sparkling from the light of the view boxes.

"Hey, what's happenin' stranger? How's your dad doing?" he asked.

"He's coming along all right but he's going into a nursing home. We can't watch him anymore," replied Megan with a half full mouth.

"That's probably for the best," Tesfaye said, "Where's Muldoon?"

"Ahhh, he took off on me a while ago. Probably went to dinner or smoke or beat up an old person," joked Megan.

"You got that right. You know, I got a great story to-"

Sean Muldoon banged the door open and pulled up a chair close to Megan, sitting on it backwards.

"How's it shakin', Ababa? Catch any fish lately?"

"No good ones," said Tesfaye, trying to pretend he wasn't anxious in Muldoon's presence.

Tesfaye was burning up inside. His mouth had dried up and his muscles tightened. He made a quick decision to leave.

"Okay. Well, I guess you two already had dinner, so I'll go back to x-ray control."

When Tesfaye's back was turned, he heard Muldoon say to him, "Well you go, girl!" Tesfaye bit his tongue and pretended not to hear it. He walked away from the Emergency Department wondering if his job was really worth all the stress. And he wondered if his job was worth fighting for. Tesfaye wasn't sure why he even cared about anything at All Saints Hospital.

Chapter 25

Sunday September 16th ER X-ray Room

Coming back to work on a gorgeous late summer afternoon was hard for Tesfaye. It didn't seem right to be stuck in a windowless x-ray department for eight hours on such a perfect day. What made it tougher still was that he missed his family in Rochester and really felt out on a limb now, like being in hostile territory. He was put at ease though, by the warm smiles he got from his co-workers for the evening shift, Megan and Kevin. He became more relaxed when he remembered that Sean Muldoon was off that night.

Tesfaye brewed fresh coffee while Kevin went to his locker to get the restored films. Megan talked a lot about her father's confusion and general condition as Tesfaye listened quietly. Returning with the films, Kevin interrupted, "Check these out." He put the films on backlit view boxes, now rarely used since the advent of computed radiography, and turned on their fluorescent lights.

"Hey man, nice job, you got the pictures!" said Tesfaye.

"Tesfaye, notice the date on this film. See here, this topogram was done the night of the CT delay when Muldoon was working. And, notice that the topogram of the male was done on a different night." Megan perked up. Tesfaye walked close to read the dates.

"Kevin, where'd you get those?" she asked. "Hey, those are CT scout films aren't they? This patient still has his glasses on. And this other one, there's a crucifix on her neck. Let me guess, Muldoon. Am I right?"

"That's what we think," said Tesfaye.

"Yeah, but we have no clue why they were done," mumbled Kevin to no one in particular. Then he spoke up. "I'll leave it to you two detectives to figure out. I've got to get over to CT. Talk to you later," Kevin said as he left.

"Later, man," said Tesfaye.

In a short while, Megan and Tesfaye moved a middle-aged man from the stretcher to the x-ray table. Recognizing that Tesfaye spoke differently, the patient asked Tesfaye where he was from.

"I've been to Africa," the man said. "I spent two years as a missionary with the Mormon Church. I was mostly in southern Sudan. Never made it to Ethiopia though. I'd love to go there someday."

While taking x-rays of his shoulder and pelvis, Tesfaye gave a brief synopsis of how the rebel groups eventually defeated the communist government; partly due to the aid of the U.S. and the fall of the Soviet Union. Then they talked a bit about current efforts to establish an African Union similar to the European Union. When the patient asked about the concept of African Diaspora, Tesfaye explained that it means different things to different groups. Basically, he said, it refers to people of African origin now living outside the continent who are interested in African development. To some people, Tesfaye continued, it implies those who fled oppression or war in Ethiopia. To still others, it included all the descendants of slaves living in the Americas.

Megan listened as she processed the images. There was so much she didn't know, she thought. They pushed the patient's stretcher back to the ER. The phone was ringing as they returned to the room. Megan handed the phone to Tesfaye and reached for her coffee.

"I got something for you. Listen to this," whispered Kevin, calling from CT. "Muldoon just called me. He begged me to switch shifts with him in CT tomorrow night. He wants to work my third shift. It sounded really important to him to be here tomorrow night." Tesfaye understood. That would put Muldoon with Koharski for the shift.

"Something must have come up, something sudden," Tesfaye said.

"Yeah, no one asks to work a third shift at the last minute just for the heck of it."

"What's going on tomorrow night?" pried Megan.

Ignoring Megan, Tesfaye implored Kevin, "We should come here tomorrow night to see what they're doing, man."

"What do you mean?" said Kevin. "When would we come? How would we know when to come?" he asked. "Wait, what's the time on those scans over there?"

Tesfaye put down the phone on the counter and pulled out the envelope. "Let's see, the male was done at two fifteen a.m. the female at two thirty-five a.m., on different nights," Tesfaye said. "Then we should come in here at two or so," Tesfaye suggested.

"Well, you know," Kevin started, "I'd like to help you out, but I if I'm working second shift tomorrow, the last thing I want to do is come here in the middle of the night."

Feeling discouraged, Tesfaye hung up. He knew Kevin didn't want to get more involved. He shoved the films into the envelope and tossed them in the garbage.

"Tesfaye, what are you doing?" Megan asked. "Don't throw those out!" She pulled the envelope out of the trashcan. "If you don't want to confront Muldoon about this I will," Megan said.

"You know I can't stand him. Did I tell you what he did to my friend Melissa?"

Tesfaye was repulsed by the story Megan told. After being jilted by Melissa, Muldoon repeatedly harassed her, even sending death threat text messages. Muldoon arranged it so that a friend would tap into her boyfriend's Department of Motor Vehicle records and then sent his records to a trucking company the boyfriend worked for. Muldoon accessed Melissa's confidential medical records and told everyone that her CT showed that she had air in her rectum. Worse than that, he sent the nursing school she attended a copy of a report indicating that she was once treated for hepatitis. Megan left no doubt in Tesfaye's mind that Muldoon had crossed the line so many times and in so many ways.

"I'll take these to Gilbert first thing in the morning," announced Megan. Tesfaye shook his head.

"Gilbert won't do anything."

"Then you know what we'll do?" she said. "Tomorrow night, you and I will come here before two in the morning and see for ourselves." Tesfaye was impressed by Megan's bravado, but he wanted her to know the dangers. Megan was not surprised to hear his story of getting pushed off the pier.

"So, Meg, are you still sure you want to get involved in this? I mean it could get pretty ugly. I don't know what's gonna happen tomorrow night."

"I'm totally sure. I would do anything to take down Muldoon. Besides, it sounds kind of exciting. Anyway, what's the worst that could happen? This is All Saints Hospital we're talking about. I was born here. I came to the cafeteria for ice cream every Saturday as a kid."

"Well then let's do it," said Tesfaye.

"Okay, let's meet at Doc Murphy's Bar at one o'clock sharp tomorrow night," Megan insisted. Tesfaye brightened. His trust in Megan had grown along with a new admiration. Here she was, he thought, basically parentless and now living alone, and willing to help a friend from work that she really didn't know that well. Tesfaye dwelled uneasily on the next night. He didn't want a confrontation yet he didn't want to let the opportunity pass either.

Chapter 26

Overcast and gray, the morning's threat of rain was a welcome thing. Days upon days of late summer hot air and humidity grated on people's nerves as much as the constant pounding of jackhammers. Tesfaye had not slept well; it seemed his leg muscles had twitched all night.

Noontime had come and gone before Tesfaye drove away from his apartment. He needed to finish research on erosion for his Soil class in the computer lab.

The erosion in the photos he reviewed at the university was nearly identical to the worn, flattened decay of mountains he grew up around. The power of water spread over millions of years could carve out the most fantastic pinnacles, arches and terraced plateaus. Tesfaye promised himself that when he next returned to Africa, he would explore those same features he once ignored.

Tesfaye put back on his baseball cap, leaned back in his chair at the computer, and spread his arms into a stretch. He saved photos and graphs on his flash memory stick and then removed the stick from the computer. He would complete the project later in the week. But for this day, Tesfaye had something more special planned, something he wanted to do for months. An occasional runner, he brought with him shorts and a shirt to change into. Once changed, he left for his car on the other side of the packed parking lot. The day was still gray but yet the asphalt radiated warmth. A red sports car slowly crept behind Tesfaye as he approached his parking spot. Tesfaye turned to look and then realized the guy just wanted his space. However, Tesfaye just threw his backpack into the trunk and waved the car past.

First walking, then jogging to warm up, Tesfaye diagonally crossed the lot to access a path leading to the university's new track stadium. By a bench under some tall pine trees, Tesfaye paused to stretch his hamstrings. He felt a moist breeze through its airy branches. Putting his hands into the ground's pine needles, he leaned forward with one leg back to warm up his hip flexors.

Now ready, Tesfaye ran down the black path to the stadium a half-mile beyond the trees. Propelled by dormant childhood dreams of becoming one of the great Ethiopian marathoners, he built up his pace and breathing to a steady rhythm. Whether it was the high altitude training, genetic predisposition or *teff*, a high-energy staple food of Ethiopians, no one knew for sure why so many great distance runners hailed from that region.

But Tesfaye now came to the real reason for this day's run, seeing what it must be like to run into a stadium from an Olympic athlete's point of view.

The terrain dropped gently as the evergreen trees opened up to reveal the massive concrete entrance. Tesfaye picked up speed, passed joggers of all shapes and sizes, and approached the open brushed aluminum gates. Running through the gates, he imagined the glory of being a super-conditioned athlete from his homeland. Tesfaye had never run on a real track before. Feeling its spongy give, he stepped up onto its red rubberized surface. Chin up and arms swinging, he stayed between the white lines of his outside lane. Though not a great runner, Tesfaye loved running on this soft new track. Now he opened up his stride, rounded the first curve and saw a flash of lightning in the distance. He burned off the adrenalin built up in his system like it was rocket fuel. The smell of rain hit his nostrils and thunder rumbled to his left. The light of the cloudy sky dimmed. A girl running in a pink outfit stood out against the grayness, reminding Tesfaye of Megan.

Around the fourth turn, Tesfaye felt the first wave of heat on his forehead beneath his cap. Perspiration followed along with large drops of random rain. A bottled-up energy store from deep within him drove him faster and faster. Darkness prevailed as if it was evening and the runners' clothes glowed in neon against it. Tesfaye felt the rain platter down on and his arms and legs. Another flash of light followed by a quick crack of thunder. Then the clouds could hold out no longer and erupted rain in diagonal sheets. Through this shower Tesfaye surged and splashed. He felt power grow within him as the cool wetness refreshed him. He ran through the rainstorm and its shower cleansed him. It washed away the blood, the vomit and the disease of working with sick people. And it cleansed Tesfaye's mind of bad memories, distant and recent.

The water poured over the brim of his hat and his green shirt was plastered to his chest. Still he ran with gliding strides, feeling his muscles flex and extend, feeling stronger than ever. He didn't stop until a streak of sunlight broke through outlined clouds and shined golden on his face. Tesfaye walked in this new light with a deep kind of strength he never felt before. It's the kind of strength that doesn't depend on what you have or who you know or even where you're from. And it can't be taught only learned. And it doesn't come overnight either. Tesfaye Ababa looked around the stadium and saw the world not in black and white, but in its myriad of colors reflected back onto the water on the track. Colors that people like Muldoon would never see. He was strong enough now. He was strong enough to open his eyes and his mouth to speak out in a world with too many children and not enough adults.

Chapter 27

The ice-cold bottles of Bud soothed Megan and Tesfaye in Doc Murphy's Bar and Grill. At one in the morning, this crusty watering hole across from All Saints Hospital was still as packed as the ER waiting room. Over the beat of the loud rock music, Megan strained her voice to tell Tesfaye a story of a guy she saw stand up on that very table in a drunken dance. From what Tesfaye could make out, Megan dated him a few times until the fateful night that he showed his true colors—namely his lime green boxers. The guy, who she said resembled a young, thinner version of Sylvester Stallone, must have recognized that Megan had lost interest in him. Their last date ended when he climbed up on their table in the middle of the crowd to dance to "She Bangs" by Ricky Martin. She walked out when he dropped his pants.

Since Tesfaye could barely hear her, his thoughts began to dwell on the night ahead of them. He wondered about essentially two things. What were they going to discover tonight? And if they do discover something illicit, then what would be the next step? Tesfaye acknowledged to himself that he really didn't have a plan. At least with Megan there, she would be a witness to it all, someone who would back him up when needed.

Over in All Saints Hospital, Koharski removed a porno video from the DVD player in the MRI waiting room. Koharski and Muldoon often "borrowed" the keys to MRI to kill time in this secluded part of the building. During the day, the TV showed either a reassuring video to MRI patients or a cautionary instructional video for employees. But on slow nights, the large screen was just like home theater for the two technologists. Earlier in their shift, they not only laughed and gawked at images of human skin, they also played their favorite game in MRI. In the game, they would bring five foot lengths of tape attached to pens, keys, pliers and a variety of metal objects and suspend them in mid-air with the power of the 2.0 tesla magnet. They stood about six and a half feet away from the gantry and just within the gauss line, the distance limit of the magnetic field. It was as if gravity had turned sideways with the magnet being the earth. The trick was to not let any object near enough to attach itself to the magnet. That would be impossible to explain to the morning MRI technologist, not to mention the repair expense and probable termination by the hospital.

Tesfaye motioned to his watch that it was time to go. Hitting the sidewalk in the now cool night air, they quietly strode across the street. Passing the main entrance, they walked to the far end of the hospital. Turning the corner, they peered into the shadows for the alley between the MRI trailer and the building. They slipped into the dark passage toward the emergency exit outside of CT. That door that was usually propped open. Stopping suddenly,

Megan spotted the orange burning glow of a cigarette tip. The exit door abruptly closed and locked. The large silhouette had been Muldoon, they guessed. Now they wondered if they had been seen. Regardless, they retraced their steps swiftly past the hospital's front towards the emergency entrance. Since they were wearing summer street clothes and not their usual hospital scrubs, they needed the help of a familiar face to get in. By waving to the old security guard, they were buzzed through the double doors of the ER. They walked past patients lined up on stretchers in the hall – a sign of another busy night.

Into the dimmed lobby, Tesfaye followed Megan's quick steps. A soft warm light illuminated the portrait of St. Teresa of Avila, an angel piercing her heart with a long golden spear. Then they entered the hall to the radiology department. When they reached the CT control room door, Megan hesitated.

"Should we just barge in there?" she asked.

"Well, Meg, I didn't come here to stand in the hall."

They found Koharski, seated at a workstation, typing parameters for the next scan. In the scanner room, Muldoon was helping a patient climb from her wheelchair onto the scanner table.

Just another night? Tesfaye wondered. Koharski acted surprised to see them. So did Muldoon. Megan stumbled through an impromptu excuse that her grandma was in the ER and might need a CT. Leaving before any questions could be asked, Tesfaye and Megan then hurried to the corridor's end where the emergency exit and the MRI trailer entrance were. Shoving the door open and then slipping into the narrow outdoor alley, Tesfaye stopped for a moment. He picked up a small rock and jammed it at the door's hinge to prevent complete closure. They continued down the dark alley, now moving more slowly. When they hit the sidewalk again, Megan hushed Tesfaye, as he was about to speak.

"Look behind you," she whispered. A white Hummer stretch limo pulled up a half block past the hospital. Getting out first and with some effort was a linebacker sized man with a black leather jacket and shaved head. He took the hand of the bleached blond woman who got out next. She was clad in a tight black pantsuit and high heels. Then out came a smallish man with shoulder length gray hair and glasses, wearing a lab coat. Last to alight was a younger man in a white warm up suit with matching cap. A chain with the palm-sized initials DR dangled from D'Rick's neck. His mother followed with the bodyguard. They were coming this way. Pulling Megan by the arm gently, Tesfaye crossed the street so they could watch from a distance.

"What the—? Who are they?" Megan asked. "I bet they're going to CT."

"Could be. Did you see that chain the guy in white has on?"

"Yeah. He looks like he's somebody—or thinks he is." Sure enough, the group disappeared into the alley. "Let's go back in," Megan suggested.

Back in the control room a few minutes later, Koharski and Muldoon finished the patient's scan while Calabrey was going over his concept for D'Rick's portrait with the rapper and his mother. When Koharski had the chance, he pulled Muldoon aside and laid into him.

"You know sometimes I think my dog has more brains than you. What were you thinking, bringing all these people in here when we still had a patient?"

"I just—"

"—Wrong answer. The answer is, you weren't thinking," Koharski growled. "And now we have Ababa and McDonnell sneaking around here. You messed things up big time, when you went around showing off that cell phone photo. You just can't help yourself, can you?"

"Listen, Ron, this is going to work out. You gotta trust me. Do have any idea how famous D'Rick is? Tonight, is gonna be awesome. We'll each make enough money to get a new jet ski. Come on, trust me dude."

"Okay. Listen, Sean, basically we have to run this ship more tightly," whispered Koharski. "Lock all the doors here and keep them locked until we're finished with these friggin' scans. Those two might come back."

"We'll be ready," claimed Muldoon holding up a large roll of duct tape.

"You gotta be kidding! Duct tape? Muldoon, this is not a kidnapping. Save that for your love life."

This time, Megan and Tesfaye found the exit door in the alley propped open. Hearts pounding, Tesfaye and Megan boldly entered the hospital corridor. But the CT control and scanner room doors were locked. Megan pounded on the door. After not getting a response, Tesfaye pulled her down the hall to talk.

"We've got to get in there. How else can we find out what they're doing?" whispered Tesfaye.

"Let's call Dave over at the security desk. He can send someone to unlock the door," suggested Megan. They found a phone and called security.

"Dave? Hi. It's Megan McDonnell from Radiology. Listen, I need to get into CT, I left my purse in there earlier and now it's locked."

"CT? I don't have anyone to send you right now. I'm short one guard tonight. One of the guys called in. Isn't Ron Koharski over there in CT tonight?" asked Dave.

"I'm not sure. All I know is, right now it's all locked up."

Megan put the phone down and said to Tesfaye, "Security is going to send someone over as soon as they can."

In the quiet of the empty radiology department, Tesfaye got impatient. "This is taking way too long. We've got to get in there now or our chance will be blown," complained Tesfaye. "Wait, if we can't get in there, maybe we can get someone to come out of there," he said.

"Explain it. What do you mean?" asked Megan softly.

"Okay, we need a reason for Muldoon or Koharski to open the door. Like having Dr. Mughari call over there and demanding one of them come to the ER immediately," offered Tesfaye.

"No, no, no. I got it. I'll call Muldoon's ex-girlfriend, Melissa. She's in my cell phone," said Megan and then she popped her cell phone open and pushed buttons. "It's ringing."

"Hello," said Melissa weakly.

"Melissa? It's Megan. Sorry to wake you up but it's an emergency. I need a really big favor. I think we finally got something on Sean. Something that will get him fired."

"Fired! Okay… Count me in."

"I need you to call him on his cell, and if he doesn't answer, call him in CT." Megan rattled off the CT extension and what she wanted Melissa to say.

Tesfaye and Megan returned to the CT corridor as soon as Megan finished the call. They stood behind a linen cart within five feet of the control room door.

Behind the locked doors, Calabrey was setting up the pose for the supine D'Rick's topogram. The rapper's capped head was turned to a profile. The gold chain with the oversized letters DR rested on his chest. Both hands held lifelike guns. D'Rick's mother, Sharon, watched the artist's meticulous preparations with curiosity. Muldoon appeared relaxed with Anthony the bodyguard standing by his shoulder. Feeling his cell phone vibrate on his side, Muldoon took the call while Koharski readied the scanner.

"Yeah? Hello?"

"Sean, it's Melissa."

"Melissa? What do you want? It's after two o'clock in the morning. I would have guessed you'd be all tucked in by now."

"Sean, I couldn't sleep. I've missed you so much."

"Right. And I'm King Tut!"

"You were right, I was wrong. Gary was a jerk; I should have never gone back to him."

"I told you so-"

159

"-Listen for a second. Sean, please come to see me. We need to talk. I'm down in the ER waiting room. Will you come over here now? Tell whomever you're working with that you'll be right back. But I've just got to see you. You know I always loved you. I'll make it up to you so good. You know I will," begged Melissa.

"Ugghhh. You drive me crazy. I'll be down in a minute," said Muldoon. Then nodding to Koharski, "Hold down the fort. I'll be right back." Muldoon got a frown from Koharski as he left the room.

Tesfaye dashed out from behind the linen cart before the door could close. Together, Megan and he jumped into the control room. Unfortunately, Muldoon spotted them, recognized the ruse and was right on their heels. He pushed Megan deeper into the room.

"Nice try kids!" uttered Muldoon, his large frame filling the doorway. "You had me goin' there for minute."

"Welcome to our little party," announced Koharski.

"And what can we do for you guys? I mean, how is grandma doing, Megan?" Muldoon asked mockingly.

"You're finished Muldoon, Koharski too. You're going to lose your license, your job and you'll be sued for negligence," Megan shouted.

"What are you talking about?" Muldoon yelled.

"Is there a problem here?" interjected Calabrey as he stepped back in, pulling the bangs from his glasses.

"Everything is under control. Are you ready for the scan, Calabrey?" asked Koharski impatiently.

"Just about," called Calabrey, now returning to the scan room.

Tesfaye took in a breath and began, "Here's what we're talking about, Muldoon. Let me spell it out for you. Negligence. Gross negligence. You see, we retrieved and printed the scans of Bethany Baird that you erased. The time marked on those scans is the same time that you said CT was down with a power failure.

At that time, you should have been scanning a real patient named Patricia Coughlin. You know man, Patricia Coughlin died because you two delayed her brain scan. You delayed the surgery that would have stopped the bleed in her brain. We can prove it."

"She would have died anyway! She was a goner. Where are those films now? You get them to me or I'll make your life a living hell, Ababa," demanded Muldoon.

"If I may make a suggestion?" inquired Calabrey from the scan room doorway. He appeared more nervous and paler than usual. The argument with its revelation of a patient death left him weak and queasy. "Sir, why don't you go get the scans in question," he said to Tesfaye. "Bring them back here and I'll write you a check for, say, twenty thousand dollars. I bet you two could make use of that."

Tesfaye rejected the offer, shaking his head. "Not going to happen, not for all the coffee in Colombia." Muldoon rose from his chair, sending it slamming to the floor. He shoved Megan aside and locked the door.

"I'm not gonna' stand back and let you interfere, Ababa," warned Muldoon. Then the brawny bodyguard put his hand on his sidearm. Together he and Muldoon herded Tesfaye and Megan into the empty scanner room. Muldoon and the bodyguard each blocked an escape route.

Tesfaye felt his heart pound. He was ready for a fight, if that was where this was headed. But Muldoon began to calm down and stood with arms folded at the doorway.

"Listen, you guys. I know we've had our differences from time to time. And I know I've made some mistakes, too. But, please can you just wait here for a few minutes until we're done with this scan! This is big money. I mean really big. Do you want in? We can work something out," pleaded Muldoon, appearing suddenly diplomatic.

In the control room, Koharski growled, "Let's move it, Calabrey."

"Almost ready," Calabrey mumbled. "I just want to—"

"—Now!" yelled Koharski. Koharski led Rod Calabrey and Sharon Perry out of the scan room to the control room. Koharski began the topograms.

"Sean, what's going on here?" demanded Tesfaye. "Obviously, these people aren't hospital patients. Bethany Baird wasn't a patient. Why the secrecy?" asked Tesfaye as he tried to peer across to the opposite scan room.

"Yeah Muldoon, just tell us what's going on and we'll decide whether to blow you in to the Department of Health!" said Megan.

"Department of Health?!" asked Muldoon incredulously. "You wouldn't do that!" Tesfaye saw Muldoon cheeks flush red and his eyes narrow with rage.

"Of course we would, you idiot!" yelled Megan. Muldoon lunged across the room toward Megan. In a soccer-like slide, Tesfaye tripped up the larger man, sending him crashing face first into the code cart. Muldoon groaned in pain, abrasions across his left forehead. With a look of apprehension, the bodyguard backed away as Muldoon staggered back up. Koharski had turned from his workstation with marked annoyance at the disruption. Tesfaye jumped over the scanner table, as Muldoon came at him. Megan screamed for Muldoon to stop and then dashed to the far wall and pulled the blue code button.

Moments later the address system announced, "Code sixty-six, CT department. Code sixty-six, CAT scan." D'Rick's mother got him immediately off the scanner.

"Babe, we got to go. We got to go now." Together they hurried from the scan room. Koharski stopped his attempts to burn the scans onto a CD and phoned the operator. According to the instructions he gave her, she announced, "Cancel code sixty-six, cancel code sixty-six, CT department."

"Hold on!" barked Koharski to Calabrey, without taking his eyes off his monitor. "I got the scans almost ready for you!" He ejected the CD from the computer and reached up to show it to

Calabrey. But the hunched artist was standing at other scan window with the others, gawking at the brawling men.

Muldoon had cornered the smaller Tesfaye between the scanner and the wall. "Give me your best shot, Ababa! Come on, you little monkey!" Muldoon taunted.

Tesfaye now boiled with a rage not felt since boyhood fistfights. He concealed it from Muldoon, though, and replied, "You first – or are you afraid, you big ape!"

Tesfaye's unruffled attitude only incensed Muldoon more. An uncontrolled blood thirst overcame Muldoon as he abruptly threw a too-high punch. Tesfaye ducked, and then dove into Muldoon's abdomen. Together they fell sideways, Tesfaye's shoulder bouncing off the scanner gantry before they struck the floor. Now Tesfaye felt the crush of Muldoon's full weight. Muldoon got one hand on Tesfaye's throat and began to choke him. Tesfaye grabbed his wrist to try to remove it. Tesfaye felt Muldoon's hot, rapid breaths on his face. As the men wrestled, Megan desperately searched for something, anything that could be used as a weapon. She quickly rejected plastic basins, a box of gloves and sponge head-holders as too light. An IV pole would be impossible to swing. Above the wall-mounted used needle container, she reached to grab a heavy, fourteen-inch pewter crucifix. Megan kissed the Jesus icon on the forehead, closed her eyes and swung at the back of Muldoon's head. When the sharp blow to his occipital bone connected, he bellowed in agony. He grabbed his head with both hands, thereby releasing Tesfaye. Then, before Muldoon could get up, she struck him again on the head. This time Megan met her mark with a debilitating force and accuracy that put Muldoon out cold. Koharski and the artist's group squirmed in horror when they saw Megan hit Muldoon with the cross. Tesfaye scrambled to his feet, and together with Megan, moved to the control room where they saw D'Rick confronting Calabrey.

D'Rick got in Calabrey's face. "D'Rick don't like this. Don't like this one bit. You told me this was legit. I told you I hated hospitals. Now get us out! Anthony, momma, come on."

"Wait, Calabrey, the money, now!" Koharski demanded. Calabrey ignored him. Tesfaye stood bewildered by these strangers in CT, still not understanding who they were. Then, hearing the name "D'Rick," it dawned on Megan who the celebrity was.

"I know who you are!" she exclaimed. "You're that rapper who sings 'Can't quit'."

But D'Rick was already halfway out the door, fleeing with his mother. He bolted down the hall with the bodyguard and artist close behind. In his haste, D'Rick missed the emergency exit and pulled his mother down through the door leading to the MRI trailer. Anthony and Calabrey followed, shouting for them to stop. Then Muldoon stumbled into the control room and sat with his head between his legs. Tesfaye reached for the phone to call security. Koharski blocked him and held down the handset.

At that moment, the rapper's mother screamed into the control room, "Come, hurry, Derrick's hurt!" Koharski, Tesfaye and Megan followed her into the MRI trailer.

Rod Calabrey and a morose-looking bodyguard stood over a motionless D'Rick, his white warm-up suit splattered with blood. His mother knelt by his side sobbing.

"The magnet pulled my piece right out of my hand. It flew right out of my hand," Anthony grunted. "It stuck to that doughnut thing," he said, pointing to the MRI scanner. "See, it's still there."

The powerful superconductive magnet, always on, held the gun solidly against it. Nothing short of a total emergency shutdown could release it from the magnetic field of over thirty thousand times that of the Earth's.

"When I tried to pull it off," he continued, "it fired," Anthony explained. Koharski stared down in disbelief at D'Rick, the plastic guns still in his hands. Tesfaye saw blood streaming from a hole in the side of his forehead. Joining the group was Muldoon, his face scratched up and looking stunned. He immediately harassed Tesfaye and Megan.

"This wouldn't have happened if you two had stayed out of it. You chased them into MR, Ababa. They shouldn't have come in here!" Muldoon complained heatedly, his eyes reddened and peering down at Tesfaye.

Tesfaye pulled out his cell phone and dialed 911 to report the accidental shooting. Once they heard that police were coming, Calabrey and the bodyguard quietly squeezed past the others, heading to the exit. Koharski felt D'Rick's neck for a pulse. "A weak heartbeat but he's still alive! Call a code. Somebody turn up the lights!"

Megan phoned in the code to the operator. Then she called hospital security. Koharski held pressure over D'Rick's wound with gauze as his mother wept.

"We should call Gilbert, too," said Tesfaye. Megan left to search for her number.

Tesfaye turned to face Muldoon. "Why don't you go back to CT in case the ER needs you?"

"Don't you tell me what—"

"—JUST DO IT!" yelled Koharski, again feeling D'Rick's neck to check his pulse.

Sharon Perry stood up and wiped her eyes. Tesfaye handed her a small box of tissues. She blew her nose as the code team ran into the room. Tesfaye tugged gently on her arm to make space for the first nurse on the scene. Kathy, Meg's sister, rushed up to the doorway, pushing a respiratory ventilator. The long bearded Doctor Mughari appeared and called out a series of short questions and commands. Koharski and a red haired nurse responded to each one.

Off to the side in the small, more dimly lit MR control area, Sharon plopped down in a chair. She opened up to Tesfaye, "Derrick was always a difficult child. He seemed to have so much anger. I still don't know why. Do you know, he used to scream

165

out 'Stop it!' in middle of the night? So when I found out that he loved rapping, I really encouraged it. He had everything a boy could want, money, cars, clothes. It's all my fault..." She trailed off into soft sobs.

Megan came back in and listened to D'Rick's mother. "His career had really started to go downhill. Bad reviews, you know. The competition on the Internet is brutal. So, I thought the CAT scan pictures would be great for marketing. You know, cutting edge medical stuff mixed in with a gangster motif," she said, barely audible over the tones of monitors, the moving of carts and equipment and the voices of the code team in the crowded MR trailer.

Tesfaye sought clarification. He asked, "D'Rick was having a CT to promote his career? His music?" Sharon nodded. "Then who were those other two guys? You know the one with the gray hair and the one with the gun?"

Megan folded her arms and Tesfaye stroked his thin beard as Sharon explained. "Oh that was our bodyguard, Anthony and Rod Calabrey, you know, the artist. I've known Rod for years. He's a creative genius. The CT art was his concept – it would have been great..." She leaned from her chair to see what they were doing for her son and then turned away in agony.

"Can I ask you something?" Megan said gently. Sharon nodded, wiping her face with a tissue. "Do you know Bethany Baird?"

"Yes, we've met. But I don't know her very well."

"Did this artist also get her scanned to make, well, a work of art?" asked Meg.

"Exactly. You should see it. It's really striking. It's as if Bethany was revealed in layers of luminescent colors. Rod is amazing." Megan raised her eyebrows and her eyes met Tesfaye's. Tesfaye made a forced smile. Then, their attention turned back to the code team.

The red haired nurse put a rigid cervical collar on D'Rick's neck. A group of three team members lifted D'Rick and carried him to a stretcher by the TV in the patient waiting area. Dr. Mughari listened for breath sounds with his stethoscope.

"Let's intubate him and get him to CT to evaluate his brain. Maybe we can see the bullet. And get a hold of the neurosurgeon on call," instructed Mughari. Kathy prepared to place an endotracheal tube down D'Rick's throat.

Dave and another hospital security guard came in with two Buffalo police, a towering officer with a shaved head and goatee and a small-framed female officer. After Kathy intubated D'Rick, the female officer followed the code team to CT while the tall officer took out his notebook and started asking questions. Tesfaye directed him to the gun still adhered by magnetism to the MR unit. Koharski left for CT with Sharon. He wanted to make sure the scan got done quickly, in case Muldoon had taken off.

The MR suite quieted as the team exited. The multiple beeping sounds and voices faded as the doors closed. Tesfaye and Megan answered more questions for the cop, who was now photographing the scene with his cell phone.

"The gun belongs to a guy named Anthony. He's D'Rick's bodyguard. He took off with the artist after the shot went off," explained Tesfaye.

"Where are those two now?" asked the cop.

"Sharon, D'Rick's mom, she would know. She just went to CT," responded Tesfaye.

Tesfaye saw Megan sitting in the dark at the MR workstation, her head down on the desk. "You okay, Meg?"

"Yeah. But I'm exhausted. All this stress burned me out."

"Why don't we get some coffee? We can sit and talk—"

"Sit and talk for a while. That's exactly what we'll do." A voice rang out. It was their boss, Ellen Gilbert, after being called in. She continued, "Come on Megan; let's get you out of here. We'll find someplace comfortable. You two need to tell me your side of the story."

Chapter 28

Tuesday September 18ᵗʰ University at Buffalo

Exhausted. Two hours sleep isn't enough, Tesfaye thought, for the concentration required for graphing the results of soil analysis. He plugged the figures from his hydrometer tests into the computer, still feeling the effects of the previous late night. He wondered how it all came down to one tumultuous night. But, then again, he knew that the tension had been building for weeks.

Tesfaye let out a long sigh. His classmate, Michael Bowman, seated at the computer next to him gave him a sideways glance. It didn't help that Megan had called him at six in the morning either. With her father now in a nursing home, she was alone in the house and frightened. She had called Tesfaye because her phone rang and a male voice said he was coming over. In her sleepy haze of confusion, Megan didn't immediately recognize the voice. She called Tesfaye, thinking it was he that called. Together, they guessed it was Sean Muldoon. Megan didn't need much encouragement from Tesfaye in order to grab a few things and drive over to her sister's house for safety.

Tesfaye continued to input his data, then allowed the program to process the results using the formulas they were given. Somehow, soil sieve and density analysis lost its earthy charm when staring at a computer monitor. Tesfaye really preferred it when his studies took him out into the natural world.

At last, he was finished for the day. His results had been charted, checked and e-mailed to his professor. He pulled his flash memory stick out of the school's computer, grabbed his backpack and waved to the last couple of classmates still in the lab.

While he walked across the expansive parking lot in the refreshingly cool air and mid-day sun, Tesfaye recalled that these were the last days of summer. The weather in September so far had been wonderful, a real relief for him from the oven-like end of August. He spotted his car, a silver Pontiac, about fifty yards away. As he turned over in his mind the probable firings of Koharski and Muldoon, Tesfaye hoped he'd never see them again. A large man in a blue windbreaker appeared to be standing by his car. No, it can't be, thought Tesfaye. A sick feeling in his stomach lasted only a few steps, however, when he ultimately realized it was a false alarm. It was not Muldoon after all.

Chapter 29

The din of the radiology department employees drowned out Ellen Gilbert's voice as she tried to begin the monthly staff meeting. This was the largest turnout she had ever seen. The only obvious absences were Ron Koharski and Sean Muldoon. After hushing the crowded room, she asked people to sit down.

Tesfaye took a seat between Ivan and Megan. He felt more relaxed than he had in a long time. Over the last few days, he kept himself busy in the classes and lab at school, as well as finishing the presentation he was about to give.

Ivan leaned over towards him. "Tesfaye, you missed our chess game on Monday. I called and left a message. What happened?" asked Ivan.

"Well, basically I totally forgot about it. Sorry about that, man. Maybe next week," replied Tesfaye, only telling half the truth. True, he did forget about going to Ivan's apartment for chess. He had other things on his mind at the time. But the rest of the story was that he'd lost interest in chess. Though he was never the competitive type, losing almost every game to Ivan wasn't fun. And there was something too cut and dried about chess, something cold and calculated. Tesfaye had other pursuits he wanted to explore. Next Monday night he would be a taking a swim class instead of playing chess. Ivan and Tesfaye turned towards the front of the room.

Ellen Gilbert finally began, "I think everyone knows what happened here the other night, but I would like to spell out some of the consequences of this incident." Essentially an introvert, Gilbert appeared stiff and uncomfortable.

"First of all, the injured singer, Derrick Perry, whom many of you know as 'D'Rick,' continues to improve in ICU. Thankfully, he is alert and breathing on his own. And luckily, the bullet ricocheted before it entered his skull. Please do not visit him or make any comments to the reporters you may have seen in the lobby. One of our neurosurgeons, Dr. Goldman, performed a craniotomy to reduce the internal pressure from the bleeding in Derrick's brain. The doctor could not, however, remove the bullet, which is lodged in what's known as Broca's area of the brain. This region coordinates the muscular movements necessary for speech. If you happen to encounter Derrick's mother, Sharon, please make any necessary interactions with her short and sweet. To put it bluntly, the hospital is in enough trouble as it is," commented Gilbert, leading a few individuals to laugh.

"Now, moving on to the consequences in MRI. All Saints will be forced to spend thousands of dollars to replace the helium coolant that was expelled from the unit during the shutdown quench of the magnet. This shutdown was needed to remove the firearm from the magnet's gantry."

"Sean Muldoon and Ron Koharski, as you already know, have been suspended without pay, pending a hospital review. It never ceases to amaze me how the occasional recklessness of two associates can wreak so much havoc. Most likely, they will lose their licenses as the Department of Health begins its

171

investigation." A couple of high fives were exchanged with this last remark, but many grumbled that they should have been fired. Additionally, a rumor was now spreading that Ellen and Sean were related.

"There is nothing humorous here," preached Gilbert. "In fact, All Saints faces a multimillion dollar negligence lawsuit stemming from an alleged delay in CT a few weeks ago. Again, be careful what you say to any attorney or reporters regarding this."

"As a final note—before we move on to the Quality Assurance presentation—in the future, please come to me when you see any unusual or disturbing behavior in the department. We could have nipped this thing in the bud with a simple conversation." Megan looked over at Tesfaye and rolled her eyes in disgust. Tesfaye smiled at her and then fiddled with his laptop.

"Okay. Today, we begin a series of presentations on quality, which Tesfaye here has kindly agreed to give. Please give him your undivided attention," said Ellen Gilbert, motioning to Tesfaye that it was his turn.

The group quieted when Tesfaye started slowly.

"Artifact awareness, easy for you to say but not for me. I hope you understand me. My English could be better."

A little laughter rolled through the crowd. He began his Power Point presentation with a bang. He projected an image of a skull x-ray with a bullet. The group murmured.

"Some artifact items can be removed and some cannot. Our job is to check for, and remove, what we can - to be sort of a detective." Tesfaye showed several remarkable images during his talk including an abdomen x-ray with pills in the stomach. The final two were of Rod Calabrey wearing clothing and glasses and then Bethany Baird with a cross, jewelry, and clutching knives. The room became noisier as laughter and commentary arose from the staff.

"Okay," said Tesfaye, trying to get everyone's attention again. "Okay, since these topograms were not done for medical reasons, I don't see why I can't share them with you, it's not a

172

HIPPA violation or anything," explained Tesfaye, referring to the medical records privacy law. After a moment while the group studied and talked about the images, Tesfaye continued.

"Instead of 'Artifact Awareness,' I actually thought about naming this talk 'Art and Artifact' instead. You see, we have so much control over the quality of our x-rays, sonograms, CTs and MRIs that it is not a big jump, I mean not a big stretch of imagination to see the art in it. And isn't it a coincidence that a known artist saw the beauty of our images. And he tried to use them to enhance his fame and fortune? I would like to suggest that we all occasionally slow down. That we slow down long enough to appreciate the pictures that we make and the knowledge we use in making them.

"And one last note, perhaps more important than anything else: When you do slow down a bit, take a look into the eyes of your patient for just long enough to realize that *they* are the reason that *we* are all here. They're putting their trust in us not only for good images, but for their health and well being too."

Tesfaye glanced over at Ellen Gilbert, turned up his hands and said, "That's all I have." He closed the laptop and went back to his seat. Megan started applauding. Kevin picked it up. Soon the whole room rippled with it, reminding Tesfaye of the patter of rain on a hard dirt road. But he wasn't hearing the start of the rainy season in his homeland. He was hearing the sounds of affirmation from friends here in America over the drumbeat of his heart. For in spite of what a small triumph this presentation was, it represented so much more. Tesfaye Ababa drank in the moment, pressing his fist to the fist of one friend, getting a pat on the back from another, and feeling the smiles of everyone upon him.

Epilogue

In a jet high over the Horn of Africa, Tesfaye stared out at the rugged plateaus and deep valleys of his homeland. There was so much of Ethiopia he hadn't seen. He never got to visit the ancient historical sites. Giant obelisks, churches carved out of rock, and castles are far from the minds of people in the midst of a war. Children surrounded by poverty don't go hunting for fossils of human ancestors in the Great Rift Valley. And families in refugee camps don't go on safari to see lions and elephants. Yet the legend was still strong, he felt. The history was rich. It drew its legacy from the early African empire of Aksum, never colonized by Europe, and once spreading from Persia to the Eastern Roman Empire. It was home to the Ark of the Covenant, the Queen of Sheba and a preserver of early Christianity.

As he put away his iPod, Tesfaye felt satisfaction that the hours on this last leg of his trip had not been entirely wasted. Since changing planes in London, Tesfaye listened with his earbuds to the story of when, in 1871, the brash American journalist Henry Stanley searched for Scottish missionary and intrepid explorer Dr. David Livingstone in equatorial Africa. What captivated Tesfaye was the attention that Stanley's bold expedition garnered from the English-speaking world at that time. Until recently, Tesfaye hadn't ever heard the fabled expression, "Dr. Livingstone, I presume." It was the claimed understated greeting that Stanley gave to Livingstone when Stanley found him

174

living along Lake Tanganyika, in what is now the Democratic Republic of Congo.

Since it was not part of his education, Tesfaye presumed that Africans did not equally share in the belief that one white man finding another *farenj* in deepest Africa was a benchmark historical event. Additionally, the credit that Livingstone was given for being the first white man to see Victoria Falls was to Tesfaye nearly the same as the honor bestowed upon another white missionary who first wrote about Niagara Falls, Father Louis Hennepin. However, he enjoyed the digital recording with all the adversity that the newspaper reporter faced for fame and fortune in attempting to rescue the quiet and good Doctor.

From the air, Tesfaye could now make out the jagged green and gray edges and flat top of Ras Dashen, Ethiopia's tallest mountain at over fifteen thousand feet. As he studied its long silhouette in the setting sun, he vowed to someday visit. Focusing past it, he then saw the huge Lake Tana near the horizon reflecting the sky's golden hues.

Finally, the aircraft approached Addis Ababa's Bole International Airport. Tesfaye was thankful that he had earned enough money and gotten the leave of absence he needed. He had wanted to come back for years, always thinking he could have spent more time in Africa, more time with his mother, grandmother and the rest. Maybe he left too soon. Maybe it would have been easier in America if he had arrived as a grown man. *But those choices weren't mine,* he thought, *and my life is pretty good now.*

As the plane taxied to its gate, he talked briefly to the well-dressed older man sitting next to him. A German citizen, he said he sold medical equipment in several countries, including Ethiopia. As they waited to deplane, the salesman explained that software updates and faster computers would revolutionize CT scans by providing quicker reconstructions.

Eventually, Tesfaye descended the portable stairway into the crisp air of that December night. Following the line of passengers, he walked the short distance across the tarmac feeling achy from the long flight. A bit of excited anticipation welled up within him as he entered the gate's glass door. He tucked his shirt into his khakis, adjusted his backpack and continued into the terminal.

Upon passing the checkpoint with security personnel in their military style uniforms, Tesfaye spotted his mother in a green and white dress. A smile beamed from her face through the crowd. And then, Tesfaye Ababa widened his eyes to see the rest of his family: cousins, second cousins, aunts and great aunts, and of course, his grandmother.

After hugs, kisses on the cheeks and continued laughter, his mother pulled him aside. She hinted that she had an attractive young woman she wanted Tesfaye to meet. In Amharic Tesfaye replied, *"Eski enayalene.* We'll see about that, mom. We'll see."

www.ingramcontent.com/pod-product-compliance
Lightning Source LLC
Chambersburg PA
CBHW020441180626
46812CB00003B/1343